Make Your Dreams Come True™

Worthy Opponents
by
NICOLE CARR

WARNER BOOKS

A Warner Communications Company

Make Your Dreams Come True™
is a trademark of Warner Books, Inc.

WARNER BOOKS EDITION

Cover photo by Bill Cadge
Cover design by Gene Light

Warner Books, Inc.
666 Fifth Avenue
New York, N.Y. 10103

W A Warner Communications Company

Printed in the United States of America

First Printing: *August, 1984*

10 9 8 7 6 5 4 3 2 1

Dear Reader,   7066434

You're very special to us. That's why we're introducing Make Your Dreams Come True™, a new line of contemporary romances.

Each time you open a Make Your Dreams Come True romance, you'll enter a whole new world. You'll meet the heroine and her friends— *and* you'll get to know the special boys in her life. Best of all, you'll have a chance to help the heroine live out her dreams, because each book in the Make Your Dreams Come True series puts *you* in charge. You may be asked to help the heroine decide which boy to go out with or which school club to join. Each time you make a choice, you will be changing the heroine's life.

Maybe some of the choices in our books will remind you of decisions you've made in your own life. If you'd like to tell us about yourself or about the choices you've made, or if you have comments and suggestions about these books, you can write to us at the address below. We're always pleased to hear from you because, to us, *you're* the most important part of the story.

Sincerely,
Kathy Simmons
Managing Editor
Warner Books
666 Fifth Avenue
New York, New York 10103

IMPORTANT:
READ THIS FIRST!

Worthy Opponents cannot be read like other books. Instead, follow these simple directions to get in on the fun.

First, begin at the beginning, just as you would with any other book. After a while you will be asked to help the heroine make an important choice. Decide which choice you want to make, turn to the page indicated—skipping all the other pages—and continue reading. As the story goes on, you will have the chance to make other choices as well. Whenever your decisions lead you to an ending, go back to the beginning and start the book all over again, this time making different decisions as you read. Keep doing this until you have read all of the stories in the book. Remember: the choice is *yours*!

Jill Farrell lifted her fine, cinnamon-colored hair off the back of her neck with her hand. Sunlight poured through the classroom windows, making the room hot in spite of the air-conditioning system. It was hard to concentrate on her social studies textbook, hard to concentrate on what Mr. Hawks, her teacher, was saying. In fact, it was almost impossible.

Jill's gaze wandered to the windows. Outside, on the flat horizon, she saw the boys' cross-country track team. The boys, mostly juniors and seniors, were running as briskly as if it were a cool sixty-eight degrees instead of a stifling eighty-two. They were too far away for Jill to recognize them as individuals, but she pictured their strong, tanned legs eating up the grassy terrain.

What you need is to really get involved with someone, fall hopelessly in love. Jill's best friend, Pam Nagle, had told her that as recently as yesterday afternoon. And although Pam's dark brown eyes had been bright with laughter when she said it, they both knew that she had been more than a little serious. And they both knew that she had been, in a way, perfectly right. Jill saw the flash of green as Pam, sitting in the desk ahead of her, shrugged her shoulders to relieve her own boredom. But how could Pam be bored? Jill wondered. Pam, lucky Pam, *was* involved with someone. She was involved with—maybe even in love with—Tim Sanderson, whom she'd been dating most of this junior year. On the surface Pam was the same as always: a loyal friend, a pixie-ish clown whose favorite color was emerald green. But inside she held a mystery that was all her own—being involved with someone, going out with the same person, and really getting to care about him.

The mystery of all that eluded Jill. It was strange because she was one of the most popular girls in school and had as many dates as she wanted. But she had never felt that special way about someone, and in these last few months it had begun to worry her. "You're just being discriminating, honey," her father had told her. But that hadn't helped much. Neither had her own logic, which told her that in such a small school the chances were good that she wouldn't find someone to fall in love with. Sometimes, though, she wondered if there was something wrong with her. Why *didn't* she feel excited about any of the boys at Westmore High?

Well, that wasn't entirely true. There *was* one boy she thought about—Toby Martin. But what girl at Westmore didn't think about Toby? Impossibly smart, clever, and as handsome as a movie star, Toby was as out of place in the little town as anyone could be. Everyone said Toby was sure to go on to greater things—a place in the freshman class at West Point, a presidency in some huge corporation, a political career. Jill believed she was bound for greater things too. The difference between her and Toby was that no one else knew she was. She would have to tell them herself, when she had time.

But in the meantime, Jill often wondered, wouldn't she and Toby make a good pair?

That was exactly what Jill was wondering when something white caught her attention. She looked across the aisle just in time to see the folded white note leave Erica Babcock's hand and travel to the hand of Terri Wells, sitting behind her. Spring madness, Jill thought, watching the dangerous escapade. It has infected the whole class for weeks now, making the students do crazy things.

Like wearing shoes that didn't match and calling it the latest style from Paris.

Like filling the principal's desk drawer with jelly beans in red and white, the school colors.

Like passing notes when you might get caught.

Jill wasn't the only one who saw what was going on. Mr. Hawks also saw the note pass from Erica's hand to Terri's. Slowly, without interrupting his lecture, he made his way down the aisle toward the two girls. Jill leaned forward just far enough to tap Pam's shoulder with the eraser end of her pencil. Pam turned her head just enough to see what was going on. Put the note away, Jill thought as Mr. Hawks came closer and closer. But Terri, unaware of what was happening, spread the note open on her desk and began to read.

Mr. Hawks looked out over the class. "What about democracy as a form of government?" he asked. "Does it put itself in danger by allowing rival philosophies to participate in the system? What do you think, Terri?" he asked, coming to a halt in front of the girl.

"What?" Terri's green eyes, framed by too much mascara, flew open in surprise. One hand reflexively covered the note she'd been reading. Jill felt sorry for her.

Mr. Hawks stretched out one hand. "Perhaps you'd like to share your reading material with us," he said. "I'm sure we'd all like a change of pace."

A nervous giggle ran through the class. Jill saw that even Bill Wyley, Terri's boyfriend, was laughing. Reluctantly Terri handed the note to Mr. Hawks.

Hawks, Jill thought, was a perfect name for their stern teacher. He was tall and rawboned, with big features and narrow blue eyes. He lived on a ranch outside of town, and his skin was polished the color of sandstone by the hard sun and the restless Texas wind.

Mr. Hawks walked toward the front of the class with the note in his hand. Holding up the piece of paper, he cleared his throat and prepared to read. The class fell silent, their laughter gone. This was too much, their silence said. This was going too far—even note passers deserved privacy. But Mr. Hawks cleared his throat and began to read. Jill glanced at Erica. She was bright red, scarlet as a lobster. Her white-blond hair, pulled back from her face in a long ponytail, showed that her humiliation went all the way to her scalp.

"'Hi, Terr,'" Mr. Hawks said in his flat west Texas accent. "'Guess what? I wangled a date with Toby M. for after school today. Told him I needed to borrow his English notes desperately. Ha ha! I'd like to borrow a lot more than that! Want to bet I can get him to ask me out? Talk about someone to die for! What a hunk, huh? Happily hunting, Erica.'"

Erica Babcock looked as if she wanted to die. Jill didn't blame her. Dying would definitely be the easiest way out of this. By the end of the day the news would be all over school. It would get back to Toby, and it would get back to Erica's boyfriend, Hal. Erica would never live this down. No, dying was the only way out, Jill reasoned.

Mr. Hawks crumpled the note and tossed it into the wastebasket. Jill knew that when class was over, there would be a scramble to retrieve the note. Someone, she was sure, would want to have it as evidence. And Erica, of course, would want to get hold of it to destroy it. "I trust we can go on with the class now," Mr. Hawks said, his voice edged with sarcasm. "That is, if it's all right with you two ladies?"

Erica and Terri, staring down at their desk tops, nodded. But before Mr. Hawks could begin the lecture again, the bell rang, signaling the end of the period. "Dismissed," Mr. Hawks said, his voice heavy with exasperation.

Just as Jill had thought, there was a scramble for the note that had been tossed in the wastebasket. Luckily for Erica, Terri's boyfriend, Bill, was the one who managed to retrieve the scrap of paper. "Hand it over," Terri demanded, "and don't breathe a word of this to anybody."

As if telling him that would do any good, Jill thought. This incident was too juicy to put a lid on. Falling into step a few paces behind Erica and Terri, Pam and Jill made their way down the hall.

"I can't *believe* Hawks read that note out loud," Pam whispered, lowering her voice a little.

"I can," Jill said. "The man has no heart. Remember when Fran Garr's older sister had him two years ago and he made their term papers due the day after the prom? I think a longhorn's got more sensitivity than he has."

"And I bet there are times," Pam said, "when his wife *wishes* she'd married a longhorn instead of him."

Jill laughed. After the tense silence of the classroom, laughing felt good. Erica, less than eight feet ahead of them, whirled around. "What do you think is so funny?" she snapped, glaring at Jill. Erica's white-blond ponytail swung forward like an angry snake. Her lips were pale where she'd bitten off her coral-colored lipstick. "Just because *you're* Miss Perfect around here," Erica continued, "just because *you're* Miss Total Popularity, that doesn't mean you can't get caught doing anything, you know. And you know what? I wish you would! I wish they'd pick on *you* for a change, instead of me."

Jill took a step backward as if she'd been slapped. "Erica, I wasn't—" she began, aware that people were staring at them.

"Oh, forget it," Erica stormed, turning around and vanishing down the hall.

"Where does she get off?" Pam said indignantly. "It's her own fault she got caught, not yours."

Jill shook her head. Her fine hair just brushed the tops of her shoulders. "I guess I should be used to Erica by now," she said.

"Get used to Erica Babcock?" Pam asked. "That'd be like getting used to a cobra."

Jill loved Pam for her loyalty. "I'm not sure Erica's quite *that* bad," she said, laughing. "It's just *me* she has it in for."

"Proof of her utter stupidity," Pam said, grinning and brushing the short, crisp wings of her dark hair back behind her ears. "Look, I've got to run to get to art on time. Call you tonight, okay? By that time," Pam added, her dark eyes gleaming with mischief, "this whole thing with Erica and Toby will be common knowledge. I can hardly wait!"

Jill said good-bye to Pam and slid into her desk in study hall fifteen seconds before the bell rang. She tried to concentrate on *Jane Eyre*, the book she was reading for English class, but she couldn't. Instead, she found herself thinking about Erica Babcock—Erica Babcock and their longtime rivalry.

It was a one-sided rivalry really. And it had started in such a silly way. Nine years ago Jill's family had moved from Houston to the tiny town of Westmore. There were only three second-grade classes in the small elementary school, and it was Jill's bad luck to land in Erica's class. Erica Babcock, with her white-blond curls and china-blue eyes, was the class's undisputed queen, and from the very first moment she regarded Jill as her natural enemy. Erica rejected Jill's attempts to be friends, and she made it clear to everyone that speaking to Jill would be looked upon as an act of high treason.

In spite of Erica's actions—or maybe because of them—Jill became an overnight success. Kids wanted to eat lunch with her, have her on their teams, and invite her to their birthday parties. "I've never seen a child make friends so easily," Jill's teacher told her mother at their first conference. "I don't quite know what it is about her."

Jill didn't quite know what it was, either, but she was glad she had friends. And she would have been glad to share those friends with Erica, to be Erica's friend herself, but Erica made a contest out of it. The big split came in junior high, when Jill was elected volleyball captain over Erica. After that, Erica wouldn't even speak to Jill. She went her own path, dropping out of a lot of school activities and hanging around with kids one or two years older than she was. When the television show *Dallas* came on the air, Erica decided she looked exactly like Charlene Tilton, the girl who played Lucy Ewing. She started wearing jeans that were a little too tight and, as Pam observed, "enough makeup to drown a camel." It wasn't a very logical metaphor, but it got the point across. Erica changed in every way she could, but one thing about her never changed—she still considered Jill her rival. And after all these years Jill had stopped trying to change Erica's mind.

"You're wonderful," Lisa Valdez said as Jill pulled the sheet of paper out of the typewriter. "I've never seen anyone write so fast in my whole life."

Jill turned and looked at Lisa, the editor of the school paper. "Does that mean we're through?" she asked.

Lisa shook her head. "I wish," she said, glancing at her watch. "I'm supposed to go for a cap and gown fitting in ten minutes, and we've still got seven columns to think about filling."

"They're having cap and gown fittings already?" Jill asked, feeling that time—spring—was slipping by more quickly than she'd imagined.

"Uh-huh," Lisa said. "In two more months they'll parole me from this place."

Jill looked up at Lisa's dark almond-shaped eyes. "I'll miss you," she said. "The paper won't be the same without you."

"Sure, it will," Lisa said, laughing. "You'll be as good an editor as I am."

"Editor?" Jill questioned, her soft brown eyebrows arching above her deep blue eyes. "I think they'll make Bobby Theison editor, don't you?" According to the rules both junior assistant editors were eligible to become the senior editor.

"Maybe they will," Lisa said mysteriously, "and maybe they won't." Then she laughed. "Anyway they won't even make the announcement until next fall. We've got plenty of things to worry about before then."

"Like how to fill seven columns," Jill said, putting a fresh sheet of paper into her typewriter.

"Right," Lisa said. "Any ideas?" Jill couldn't think of anything. Ideas weren't her strong point. Once someone gave her an idea, though, she could write pages and pages about it, and those pages seldom needed more than a few light corrections. "We could write up that incident about Erica's note," Lisa said at last. "*That* certainly was news."

"Please," Jill said. "If I hear that story one more time—"

"You're right," Lisa said. "Old news."

"Let's let it die a natural death," Jill begged.

Lisa grabbed a handful of notices. "These are the spring calendar events," she said, sorting through them. "Maybe we can make a story out of one of them."

"Maybe," Jill said doubtfully. "Which one?"

Lisa read the notices aloud. "Forgiveness Day for overdue library books, hall monitors' meeting, yearbook orders being taken. No, no, and *no*! Hey, wait, what about this—filing deadline for candidates for class president elections?"

Jill froze. "What about it?" she asked.

Lisa stared at her. "Don't you see? We find out who's going to run and write profile stories about them." Jill didn't say anything. "What's wrong?" Lisa asked. "I think it's a great idea."

Jill cleared her throat. "It *is* a great idea—I just don't think I can write the story, that's all."

"Why not?"

"Well, I'm not sure yet," Jill stammered. "I mean, I haven't exactly made up my mind. . . ."

"What? *What?*" Lisa asked impatiently.

"Well, I was thinking of running. Myself, me."

Lisa's black eyes flew open. "You? That's wonderful, Jill," she said, patting her favorite assistant editor on the shoulder.

"I haven't made my mind up for sure," Jill repeated insistently. "It's just that, if I do run, I can't very well write stories about my opponents, can I? I mean, that would be unfair use of the media, wouldn't it?"

Lisa motioned Jill's worries aside with her hand. "Look," she said, "we'll get someone else to do the stories. That way, you can think it over. After all," she said, glancing at the slip of paper, "you've got four days till the final deadline." Lisa leaned back against the desk. "Whew," she said. "At least we found something for those seven columns—and I've still got time to make my cap and gown fitting."

Jill stopped Lisa on her way out of the room. "Promise me one thing," she said.

"Sure," Lisa replied, "what's that?"

"Since I haven't made my mind up about running, don't tell anyone about this, okay?"

Lisa nodded and left the room. Jill stared at the blank sheet of paper in the typewriter. Now that someone else was going to be doing the campaign profiles, she didn't have anything to write. Maybe she shouldn't have told Lisa that she was thinking about running for senior class president. Just yesterday she'd almost decided not to run. After all, it would be a huge amount of work no matter how things turned out. First there would be the campaign *and* the risk of losing to whoever decided to run against her. And what if she won? Being class president was a big responsibility. It would cut her free time down to zero. Lisa had hinted that she might be chosen senior editor of the paper—a post she would certainly have to turn down if she won the election. But in spite of everything, there was the reason that had tempted Jill to run in the first place: She believed she would be a terrific class president.

Jill was still staring at her typewriter when she felt a presence behind her. She swiveled in her chair and found herself looking up at Toby Martin. His eyes, as blue as turquoise in his tanned face, crinkled up at the corners in a smile. "Hi," he said.

"Hi, Toby," Jill answered. "Lisa's not here right now. She'll be back in a few minutes though. Or maybe I can help you."

"Maybe you can," Toby said. "I've got a scoop for the paper, and I thought you might like to know about it."

For a second Jill wondered if he was referring to Erica's note. No, of course, he wasn't, Jill assured herself. Toby had too much class for that. He had handled the whole episode beautifully, meeting Erica after school as he had promised and giving her his English notes. He'd never even mentioned the note to Erica or anyone else. As far as Toby was concerned, the note simply didn't exist. "So you've got a scoop for us, huh?" Jill said playfully, returning his smile.

"I hope so," Toby said.

Jill poised her fingers over the typewriter keys and

looked at the blank sheet of paper. *Now* she had something to write about. "Okay," she said, "shoot."

"I just came from the office," Toby said. "I was the first candidate to file. I'm running for president of next year's senior class."

Jill had seen a flash flood once, had seen the way the water came tumbling over the dry land, sweeping everything in front of it. That's how Toby's words came to her—like a flash flood, sweeping a hundred different thoughts through her mind at once.

If I hadn't told Lisa I might run, I'd be assigned to interview Toby.

If I run, I'll be running against him.

If I run.

Toby stared down at her, at her hands, motionless on the keyboard. "Want me to type it for you?" he said gently. "Toby Martin—T-o-b-y M-a-r-t-i-n—for president."

When Jill looked up, she saw that he was smiling at her. "I think I'll remember," she said. "That's not the kind of news item you need to write down."

"Oh," Toby said. He leaned against the desk. "Well, that brings me to the second half of this visit, I guess."

"You have more news?" Jill asked.

Toby shook his head, and a lock of dark blond hair curled forward on his forehead. "Uh-uh," he said. "No more business. This is personal."

Personal? Jill looked at Toby. What was going on? All of a sudden, she felt confused. "How personal?" she joked. "Do you want me to leave the room?"

Toby smiled, but he didn't laugh with her. Instead, he shook his head. "No, I don't want you to leave the room," he said. "I want you to be my campaign manager."

Jill dropped back in her chair. "What?" she asked, giving her mind time to clear.

"I've thought it over, Jill, and you're the only one who could do it. There'll be lots of things to write—statements, speeches, things like that—and you're the best writer in the school. So you see, I need *you*—no one else. Just you." Toby rested his hand on her shoulder. She felt the warmth of his body seeping into her, flowing through her like sunlight. Being Toby's campaign manager—that would certainly give her a chance to get to know him, wouldn't it? And the way he was looking at her made it clear he was more than a little interested in getting to know her too. "What do you say?" he asked. "Is it a deal?"

Jill pulled away from Toby. His hand slid off her shoulder. "I don't know," she said. "I mean, I'll have to think about it."

Toby looked disappointed but he managed to smile. "Sure," he said. "Take your time. Take as much time as you need, as long as your answer is yes." Toby turned and walked out of the room, almost bumping into Lisa as she came in.

"What happened while I was gone?" Lisa asked. "Anything earth-shattering?"

Nothing much, Jill thought. The earth fell a few degrees off its axis, that's all. "I'll fill you in," she told Lisa.

Working with Toby as his campaign manager or running against him for class president? What a choice! Jill sighed. For the first time in her life she liked a boy well enough to want to get to know him better—a lot better. But feeling that way was making life harder, not easier. Rats! Hallelujah! Rats *and* hallelujah! Why hadn't anyone told her it would be like this?

♡

If you think Jill decides to become Toby's campaign manager, go to page 15.

If you think Jill decides to run for senior class president herself, go to page 33.

Jill stood in her family's den, a big room that looked out onto the side lawn. Through wide curtained windows she could see the row of plum trees that swooped along the road, their branches heavy with blossoms.

Turning away from the window, Jill surveyed the den with a critical eye. Until now she had never worried about the way the house looked. She adored her room, of course, with its apple-green walls and white furniture, but she had always taken the rest of the house for granted. Not tonight though. Tonight Toby was coming over to work on his victory speech with her. Tonight everything had to be perfect.

And it was. Well, it *almost* was. There was one tiny little problem, and Jill was looking right at it—a framed photograph of herself at age seven. The picture showed a girl with missing baby teeth, a cowboy hat dipping low over her eyes, her feet tangled in a lariat. She reached up, removed the picture from the wall and slid it behind a row of books. Now, she thought, everything really *was* perfect.

She glanced out the window again, hoping to see Toby's headlights shining through the twilight. Little hammers of excitement tapped against her veins. They'd been working on the campaign for almost a month now—the election was only a few days away, and Toby seemed sure to win. Jill was more convinced than ever that Toby—handsome, extraordinary Toby—was the only boy within a hundred miles who could coax her reluctant heart into anything even faintly resembling love. What was wrong, then? Jill wondered for the thousandth time. Why hadn't she fallen in love with Toby, and why hadn't he fallen in love with her? For the thousandth time, she offered herself the answer: time. The two of them simply hadn't had *time* to get their relationship started.

From the minute Jill had accepted the job of managing Toby's campaign, she had been kept busy writing position papers—which appeared in the school newspaper—and speeches—which Toby delivered with great flair at student body meetings. They often met at school but always with business to discuss and always with other campaign workers around. Not exactly the stuff romance is made of, Jill told herself. Tonight was going to be different though. She was sure of that. So sure, that she'd put on her favorite outfit—bright aqua pants and a striped top that skimmed her waistline, revealing a narrow stripe of early tan.

Jill continued to gaze out the window, watching purple night fall over the broad, still landscape of northeastern Texas. Suddenly there was a clattering sound behind her. Jill turned and saw her sister, Penelope, standing in the doorway. Penny was thirteen, an inch taller than Jill, and as thin and spare as a bleached bone. She was wearing her usual outfit, Jill noted—cowboy boots, faded jeans, and an oversize T-shirt. She looks, Jill thought, like an ironing board with shoulder blades.

"Hiya," Penny said, clomping across the floor in her heavy boots and flopping down on the couch. She held the *TV Guide* in one hand. She let it drop open, twisting her head sideways to read the listings.

"Oh, great," Jill heard her say. "*Dynasty* is coming on."

"Yuck," Jill said, reverting to their childhood language.

"Yuck, nothing," Penny said, eying the television set defensively. "I'm going to watch it."

"Not in here, you're not," Jill replied.

"Why not?"

"I told you at dinner," Jill said. "Toby Martin is coming over tonight so we can work on his victory speech—"

"So *you* can work on him, you mean," Penny said.

Jill flinched. "Shut up, Opie," she said. She hadn't stooped to calling her sister that in years. "It's none of your business."

"Don't call me Opie," Penny shrieked.

"Then leave me alone. Toby'll be here any minute. Why can't you go watch *Dynasty* on the kitchen TV?"

Penny made a face. "In black and white? No way. How will I know what Alexis is wearing?"

Jill felt her patience wearing thin. "Who *cares* what Alexis is wearing?" she replied, her voice rising.

Mrs. Farrell appeared in the doorway. "What's the problem?" she asked. "I can hear you girls halfway to Abilene."

"She knows Toby's coming over," Jill said, pointing an accusing finger at her sister, "and she wants to sit here and watch *Dynasty*."

"I think somebody's going to kill Alexis tonight," Penny put in.

"Oh, stop it," Jill said. "Nobody's going to *kill* Alexis."

"They might," Penny insisted. "And I want to see it in color."

Mrs. Farrell looked at them. "I don't even know who Alexis is," she said, running a hand through her short auburn hair. She glanced at her younger daughter. "Is your homework done?"

"Hours ago."

"Then you can watch the TV in our bedroom," Mrs. Farrell said. "Just one hour though—and keep those boots off the bedspread."

"Sure, Mom," Penny said cheerfully. She gave Jill a look of triumph as she clomped out of the room.

Just in the nick of time, Jill thought. Because outside, in the full darkness, she saw Toby's headlights turn into the driveway.

"I'm sorry I'm late," Toby said with a sheepish but somehow still dazzling grin when Jill answered the door. "I got caught up with something."

"That's okay," Jill said. "Come on in, won't you?" As Toby stepped by her, Jill caught the faint smell of after-shave. That was just one of the things she liked about Toby. Any other boy would have shown up in jeans and a T-shirt, probably without even showering. But Toby was wearing tan pants and a freshly pressed shirt. It was obvious that he had taken time to dress for their meeting. "I thought we could work in the den," she said casually, leading him through the house.

It took Jill twice as long to write Toby's victory speech as it would have under ordinary circumstances— ordinary circumstances, of course, being any situation in which Toby wasn't around to distract her. Fortunately Toby wasn't aware of this. Even at half speed, Jill was unusually quick.

"You're super," Toby said, reading a page as it

came out of the little portable typewriter that sat on the den desk. "Absolutely super."

Jill looked up. Toby's blue eyes were gleaming. Not at her though—they were fixed on the page of print he was holding in front of him. "Thanks, Toby," she said, and continued typing.

When they were both satisfied with the finished speech, Jill pushed her chair back, stood up, and stretched.

"Are we finished?" Toby asked.

"Unless you don't like it," Jill said. "Is there something in it you want to change?"

"No," Toby said. "No, I think the speech is terrific. But," he added, his blue eyes giving off sparks of light, "what if I lose? Hadn't we better do a concession speech, just in case?"

Jill laughed. "I don't think there's much chance of your losing. According to my chief source, you're way ahead of the opposition."

"And who," Toby asked, "is your chief source?"

"I can't reveal that," Jill said. "Highly placed and very reliable though. Trust me." Her source, of course, was Pam Nagle—Pam, who always seemed to know things ten seconds before they actually happened. There was no reason to reveal that to Toby though, Jill decided. She preferred to remain mysterious about the whole thing. "If you lose," Jill added lightly, "you'll just have to extemporize."

"Uh-oh," Toby said, laughing, "then they'll all see how much I need you. Without a Jill Farrell speech in my hand, I'm just another raving lunatic."

"A *handsome* raving lunatic," Jill corrected. The word slipped out by accident. She hadn't meant to let him know how handsome she thought he was, and now that she had, she bit her lip and looked away from him.

But it was okay—good even. Toby touched her arm to get her attention. "Can I quote you on that?" he asked.

Jill looked up. His vibrant eyes were gazing steadily at her. The warmth from his hand radiated through her entire body. This is how it happens, she thought. This is how it feels. This is the beginning of falling in love. She couldn't believe it. She felt dizzy and sick and wonderful all at the same time. She even heard bells ringing in the distance. But the bell, it turned out, was her own telephone. A minute later her mother appeared in the doorway and told Toby he had a call.

While Toby was out of the room, Jill planned the rest of their lives. College together naturally, and then jobs for both of them. A big wedding and eventually two children. They would have to move away from Westmore, of course—their careers would be much too big for the tiny little town. But the corporate jet Toby's company gave them would allow for plenty of trips back and forth. It was perfect, and Jill had never dreamed it would be so easy.

She was in the jet, learning to fly, when Toby came back into the room. "I've got to go," he said, scooping up the finished speech and offering her an apologetic smile. "There's—uh—kind of an emergency I've got to take care of."

So reliable, so responsible, Jill thought. It would be much the same when he was a corporate genius, called to Europe in the middle of the night to solve some international banking crisis. Jill smiled. "I understand," she said.

But after Toby left, she felt let down and disappointed. Her mother came into the room with a plate of food. "I made some banana bread," Mrs. Farrell said. "I didn't know Toby would be leaving so soon."

"Neither did I," Jill said. "Neither did *he*, in fact. It was some kind of emergency or something, I hope nothing serious. Did it sound like his mother?"

Mrs. Farrell hesitated. "Not really, although I suppose it could have been."

Jill said nothing. In her heart she had the sinking feeling that Toby's caller had been a girl. A girl who, like herself, had visions of a perfect life with Toby.

"So what do you think?" Jill asked Pam, picking up her untouched tuna fish sandwich. She had just finished telling Pam, in vivid detail, everything that had happened the night before. It had taken twenty-three minutes of their half-hour lunch period. Pam was going to have to deliver a verdict in record time, but Jill wasn't worried—Pam, expert on love, was the person who could do it.

But Pam hesitated. "First," she said, "tell me what *you* think."

Jill laid the sandwich, with one bite missing, back down. "I thought I just told you what I think," she replied. "I think I could fall in love with him. I think *he* could fall in love with *me*."

Pam sighed. "Forget about what you think *could* happen," she said. "Think about what *is* happening. You've been working with him a whole month, Jill. Have you fallen in love with him?"

"No," Jill said.

"Has he fallen in love with you?"

"No."

"Well, then, you see what I mean."

"But we haven't had *time*," Jill protested.

Pam shook her head. "Love isn't like a dentist's appointment, for heaven's sake," she said. "It isn't something you set aside time for and get taken care of in one sitting, like a little filling. It's something that happens a little bit at a time, and it happens whether you have time or not."

Jill finished her sandwich and began crumpling up the plastic it had been wrapped in. "How do you know?" she asked, more irritated than she should have been because she suspected there was more than a grain of truth in Pam's words.

Pam was mysterious. "It doesn't matter how I know," she said. "I just know. Believe me, if you and Toby were meant to become an item, you'd be on the way by now. That's all there is to it."

Jill glanced at her watch: 12:29. Pam had delivered her fatal judgment in six seconds flat. Jill had one minute to make her appeal. "Even if you're right," she began, "and I'm not saying that you are, but even if you *were*, what am I supposed to do about it?"

"For one thing," Pam said, her dark eyes sympathetic, "you can stop waiting on a sheep that's not going to grow wool."

"What?" Jill asked.

"Stop putting your energy into something that isn't going to pan out. You gave it a shot, helped him with the election—you've done enough. Why don't you do something different for a change?"

Jill stood up. "Like what?" she asked.

Pam picked her tray up. "Well, Tim's playing baseball this afternoon," she said, "and there's going to be a kind of picnic supper after the game. Why don't you come along?"

Jill wrinkled her nose. "I know every single boy on that team. You've got the only one worth getting."

Pam put her tray on the conveyor belt and looked at Jill. "You know, for someone who's considered pretty popular in this school, you can be a real pain in the behind."

Jill laughed. Pam had a point. "Okay," she said. "I'll come. Thanks for asking me."

"Now," Pam said, "if I could only coax you into sitting through the game with me."

"Not today," Jill said. "I've got to write a story for the paper after sixth period. Besides, I was unclairvoyant enough to wear a dress today. I want to run home and change. I'll be back for the last inning though."

"Okay," Pam said. "See you."

At home Jill slipped into cuffed khaki shorts and a plaid short-sleeved shirt. She divided her hair into two pigtails and decided against reapplying her makeup. Instead, she dabbed on a bit of lip gloss, mostly to protect her mouth from the sun. The operation took about ten minutes. What was the use of elaborate preparations? she asked herself. She knew every member of the Westmore baseball team by heart; she had known most of them since she was in the second grade. And for all the romance they offered, she might as well borrow one of Penny's ragged T-shirts to wear. If Toby was going to be there, it would be a different story, of course. But Toby wasn't going to be there. She wasn't even sure where Toby was just now. Probably caucusing with some very attractive, very available constituent, Jill thought miserably.

The game was two outs away from over when Jill arrived. She spotted Pam in the bleachers and waited for the game to be over, which it soon was—with a grounder to first and an outfield fly. The bleachers emptied, and Pam came down to meet her, rubbing the seat of her jeans and frowning.

"Those bleachers get hard after the first two hours," Pam said. "I hope Tim appreciates this. I hope he knows what I'm going through all for the sake of love."

"Want me to mention it to him?" Jill asked. "Maybe he'll get you a pillow or something."

The two girls walked away from the playing field toward the parking lot. Pam had borrowed her mother's car for the day since the picnic was being held at Lost Lake Park. "Aren't we going to wait for Tim?" Jill asked as Pam unlocked the car doors.

Pam shook her head. "He has to shower and stuff first. He'll come on the team bus. Hey, we've got plenty of time. Want to swing by Minty's and see what's new? It's not every day we have wheels, after all."

Jill nodded. Minty's was the one—and only—store in town that had clothes that even approached being fashionable. The other stores were loaded with western wear and the kinds of skirts and blouses Jill wouldn't be caught dead in. But to their disappointment Minty's offered nothing new that day. The only thing Jill saw of interest was a short pink-and-gray striped sweat shirt dress, gathered at the knees and meant to be worn with tights. "I suppose pink and gray will be out of style by the time I could get this off layaway," she speculated, fingering the price tag. "I don't see how a sweat shirt—a *sweat shirt*, for heaven's sake—can be so expensive."

Pam looked over her shoulder at the price tag and did a double take. "Well," she said, "we wear about the same size. I suppose we could always start buying clothes and sharing them. Come on, Jill, let's go before we do something crazy, like rob the place."

The smell of sweet smoke from charcoal and hickory chips hung in the air over the Lost Lake parking lot. Jill saw that the picnic area was mobbed with people, a lot more than she'd expected. "I thought there were only nine players on a baseball team," she said to Pam.

Pam rolled her eyes at her. "There's the second-string team too, you know. *And* the competition. Don't forget them. They usually show up at these things too."

"Even though they lost?"

Pam laughed. "Are you kidding? When there's free food at stake, these guys would walk on hot coals."

Jill laughed with her. She tried to remember the name of the opposing team and finally recalled it—the Alta Vista Cardinals . She wondered if she knew anyone from Alta Vista. It was a small town, after all, and not all that far from Westmore. When she searched her mind, however, she drew a blank.

"There's Tim," Pam said. "I'm going to go rag him about that error he made. Want to come along?"

Jill shook her head. "I think I'm going to find a soda and walk around for a while."

Pam took off through the crowd. Jill saw her run up to Tim and embarrass him by kissing him on the back of the neck while he was talking to his coach. She was still watching when she heard a voice behind her say, "Hi, Jill."

Jill turned and saw Rick Davis. "Hi, Rick," she said. "Did you play today? I missed all but the last inning of the game."

Rick looked disappointed. Then his broad pink and white face, tinted red where the sun had burned his nose, expanded in a slow smile. "Gosh, Jill, you missed just about my best game of the season. The first inning I was up, see, and the count went to three and two and..."

Jill listened patiently until Rick got to the bottom of the fourth inning. Her legs were falling asleep just listening to him. Besides, she was dying of thirst. At last she managed to excuse herself and get away, saying that she had to find Pam.

She didn't look for Pam though. Instead, she made her way to one of the hugh coolers that contained cans of soda floating in ice and water. She peeled the metal tab back and a geyser of root-beer foam jetted into the air. Jill held the can at arm's length. Too late, she saw that the spray of foam was soaking the unknown boy who stood beside her.

"Gosh, I'm sorry," she said sincerely, looking at his spotted shirt.

He grinned at her. He had very short dark hair and very white even teeth. And nice eyes, she noticed. Very nice eyes—a rich dark brown. "That's okay," the boy said. "I needed to cool off. It was a pretty hot game."

"You played?" Jill asked, not wanting the boy to move away from her.

"Sure did," he answered. "I'm not surprised you don't remember me though—I was zero for three at bat." He grimaced, drawing his straight dark brows together. "Not exactly one of my better days."

He and Jill had moved away from the crowd at the coolers. They stood in the shade of a big oak tree. "You must be from Alta Vista," Jill said, sipping her root beer now that it had stopped bubbling. "I mean, I'm from Westmore, and I know everyone in the whole school; have for years. So if I don't know you"—she paused and smiled at him—"you're either an Alta Vista baseball player or an alien who's infiltrating this party to study the ways of earth people."

The boy laughed. "I think I'll take the fifth amendment on that one," he said. "In the meantime you can call me Dennis—Dennis Rhodes."

Jill introduced herself and there was a moment of silence during which neither of them knew quite what to say next. Then Dennis reached out and grasped the can of root beer, his fingers brushing against hers in the process. "Regular or diet?" he asked, turning the can so he could read the label.

"What?" Jill asked. "Oh, diet."

"Good," Dennis said, pulling his still-wet shirt away from his body. "No sugar. I won't attract any flies."

Jill laughed. By the time the food was ready, she and Dennis had decided to eat together. They filled their plates with hot dogs and potato salad and pickles and looked around for a place to sit. Jill saw Pam waving to her from a picnic table. "Want to meet my friends?" she asked Dennis, and he nodded.

"I remember you," Dennis said when Jill introduced him to Tim. "You're the third baseman who threw me out my second time at bat. Glad to meet you."

The two boys shook hands. Pam shot Jill a questioning I-can-hardly-wait-to-hear-how-all-this-happened look and gave Dennis an approving glance. Jill settled herself at the table and reached for a fresh can of soda.

"Uh-oh," Dennis said, laughing and shielding himself with his hands. "Umbrellas, everyone. She's absolutely lethal with those things."

Jill opened the can very carefully. "I *can* open these things right when I have to," she said. "I only use the explosive method when I want to make an impression."

Dennis held her gaze for a moment. "Well, you certainly did that," he said.

"Was I right or was I right?" Pam asked Jill on the phone later that night. "Didn't you have an absolutely, certifiably, astoundingly *terrific* time today?"

"Yes," Jill admitted. "I did."

"And who do you have to thank for it?"

"Dennis Rhodes."

Pam paused in mock anger. "Well, that's gratitude for you," she said. "Who talked you into coming along in the first place?"

"You did," Jill confessed. "Thanks, Pam. I really *did* have a great time."

"And Dennis?"

"Oh, I think he had a pretty good time too," Jill replied. Dennis had had such a good time, in fact, that he'd wanted to kiss her good-bye before he got on the team bus and headed back to Alta Vista.

"I think he's really nice, Jill."

"Who?" Jill asked playfully.

"Dennis, of course. You do like him, don't you? I mean, you'd be nuts not to."

"I like him," Jill said. She saw no need to tell Pam everything that was going on in her mind. That, she was afraid, might make it less exciting or less important.

"Do you think he's going to ask you out?"

"Yeah," Jill said. "I think so. Of course, I might ask him out first."

"What do you mean?" Pam wanted to know.

"Well, the elections are next week, you know. And if Toby wins—"

"Which he is definitely going to," Pam put in.

"Okay, okay—*when* Toby wins, I'm sure he's going to have a victory party. I could ask Dennis to come with me, couldn't I?"

"Terrific," Pam said. "How are you going to get hold of him?"

Jill chuckled. "That's the easy part. Before he left, he asked for my number."

"So?" Pam asked. "What if he doesn't call?"

"Well, I didn't just *stand* there," Jill said. "I asked for his number too. We traded."

Pam was satisfied at last. "Good work," she said. "I'll see you tomorrow in school."

The more Jill thought about asking Dennis to Toby's party, the more convinced she was that that was what she wanted to do. Dennis was nice, and he seemed like a lot of fun. Best of all, he wasn't from Westmore—he was someone totally new. Why not see what would happen? She went to sleep with that thought in her mind, and woke up the next morning thinking about Dennis's nice smile.

Jill felt the tension and excitement in the air. It was so intense, it pressed against her in all directions, squeezing her body until her heart beat faster in response. She looked at Toby, who was standing next to her. He was as cool as a cucumber. His shirt collar was smooth and crisp. His dark blond hair reflected the fluorescence of the overhead lights. His eyes, Jill thought, were as blue as—bluer than—Paul Newman's. And they were perfectly calm and confident, Jill saw. There wasn't a trace of nervousness in them.

It was eight-twenty-three in the morning, and they were standing in the room that had been made into Toby's campaign headquarters. In exactly two minutes, when the morning announcements were made, they would know who was going to be the next year's senior class president. As recently as last night Pam had still been certain that Toby had a sizable lead. But even Pam couldn't know for sure. The votes were counted in secret by seven members of the faculty who were disgustingly above corruption.

Now that the moment was at hand, Jill was worried. What if something went wrong? What if Toby lost the election, and all her hard work for him amounted to nothing? An electronic hum filled the air as the vice-principal, Mr. Daily, switched on the microphone in his office. Jill held her breath and glanced at Toby. He reached over and squeezed her hand. "Hey," he said, "don't worry so much. It's only a school election after all."

Only a school election! Jill thought. After all the

work they'd put into the campaign? How could Toby be so casual about it?

But before Jill had time to do much wondering, the election results were read. The two lower grades came first—upcoming sophomores and juniors that nobody really cared about. It was the senior class that was important. All the students in the campaign office stopped what they were doing. They didn't breathe again until Mr. Daily read, "And in the senior elections, Toby Martin is the new class president."

A whoop of joy went up around the room. "We did it," people called out, and "Congratulations, Toby," and things like that.

Toby's eyes, so cool a moment before, were dancing. They beamed light at everyone they landed on, and right then they had landed on Jill. "Gosh," he said, "I did it—I really did it! I won!" Impulsively be grabbed Jill and drew her to him. "This is just terrific," he said, and kissed her. It wasn't a kiss on the cheek, either—he kissed her right on the mouth, right through her berries-and-cream lip gloss.

An electric current went through Jill. She didn't think she heard a word Toby said, just felt the impact of his kiss. *Pam's wrong*, she thought. *She's wrong about Toby and me, and I was right all along—all we need is the right time and the right place.*

Jill waited all day for the impact of Toby's kiss to wear off, and it did—but not completely. She was confused, and she didn't know what to do. On one hand she did agree with Pam: it was foolish to go on hoping that a relationship would develop between Toby and her. On the other hand the lingering electric spark of his kiss seemed to argue a whole other side of the story. So when Toby announced his victory party for the following Friday night, Jill wasn't sure what she was going to do. Should she ask Dennis, as she'd planned, or should she go alone, make herself available to Toby, and hope that lightning would strike?

♡

If you think Jill asks Dennis to the party, go to page 51.

If you think Jill goes to the party alone, go to page 69.

The campaign for senior class president began one Monday morning in the office of the vice-principal. Jill, Toby, and Kathy Sorensen, the third candidate, were officially gathered together for the first time. After the vice-principal read the morning announcements, each of the candidates was introduced to the student body. Jill had the bad luck of going first. Realizing that her voice was being piped into every classroom in the entire school made her nervous. She only hoped she didn't sound as ill at ease as she felt.

When Jill finished, Toby smiled and winked at her. She hadn't seen him since the day she'd told him she couldn't be his campaign manager because she was running for president herself. She still remembered the look of surprise in his blue eyes. But he'd lost little time in congratulating her on her decision. "It's nice to know that, in case I lose, the senior class will *still* get a good president," he'd said enthusiastically.

Jill stood up, and Toby slid into her place behind the microphone. "Good morning," he said calmly, "I'm Toby Martin and I'm running for senior class president. Now, no matter what you may think of me on a personal note, you have to admit I've got courage—I'm running against two of the smartest girls in class."

Jill looked at him. He wasn't nervous, she saw—not even the least little bit! The words rolled out of his mouth as easily as if he were talking to a friend on the telephone. Toby, she saw at once, was going to be a hard candidate to defeat.

Kathy Sorensen was the last candidate to introduce herself. Jill hadn't planned on having to run against two candidates, but Kathy, as Pam lost no time in pointing out, wasn't much of a threat. "She's too much of a brain to win," Pam had said. Well, that wasn't it, exactly. You couldn't really be *too* smart, Jill thought. Kathy's problem was that she was *only* smart. She didn't belong to any of the school clubs because she was too busy studying all the time, and she never went to school dances or parties because she thought they were frivolous. "She thinks the rest of us are a bunch of peasants," Pam said. "Who's going to vote for someone like that?" Jill had to agree. If personality had anything to do with getting elected, Kathy was running with a big handicap.

After they had finished in the vice-principal's office, the candidates went back to their first period classes. Kathy wished them luck and made a right turn, toward the math and science wing of the building. Jill and Toby found themselves walking down the hall alone together. Toby looked at her, his eyes sparkling. "Why do I get the feeling," he asked, "that this is going to be an unusually interesting campaign?"

Jill played along with him. "Is it?" she asked teasingly.

Toby laughed. "I can see you're on your way to becoming a politician already."

"What do you mean?"

"Answering a question with a question. It's a good trick. But in answer to your question—yes, I do think this is going to be an interesting campaign.

Very interesting. I hope we get to know each other better because of it."

Jill smiled at him. "Me too," she said. "I'd like that."

Running for senior class president, Jill discovered, was a lot more complicated than putting your name on a ballot and seeing how many of your classmates voted for you. Suddenly there didn't seem to be enough hours in the day. Just getting her platform together turned out to be an enormous amount of work. Was she for relaxing the dress code or keeping it the same? Should seniors be allowed to leave the campus during lunch period? Was there any way to make more parking space available to students?

There was no way she could handle the whole campaign alone. And luckily she didn't have to. Pam slid into the role of campaign manager, keeping her fingers on the pulse of public opinion, and a dozen other kids volunteered to help make posters and distribute leaflets. Jill was glad to have their support and was touched that so many kids she'd been friends with came through to help her when she needed it most.

Even so, most of the responsibility fell to Jill herself. *It's a good thing I don't have a boyfriend,* she thought. *I'd never have time to see him. I hardly even have time to eat and sleep.* It was no exaggeration. It was true. Today, for example, she and Pam were supposed to go over a batch of interview questions during lunch. Jill hurried toward the cafeteria, well aware that she was almost ten minutes late. Not much, maybe, but when your entire lunch period was only thirty minutes long, it made a big difference. She grabbed a tray, rushed through the line, and paid for her meal. She scanned the crowded cafeteria like a hawk but couldn't spot Pam anywhere.

Jill sat down and began eating. *I can't believe it,* she thought. *Pam's even later than I am.* Well, at least she'd get to eat her lunch. She twirled the lank, lukewarm spaghetti around her fork and lifted it toward her mouth. Just as she began to chew she glanced up and saw Toby, his lunch tray in his hands.

"Hi, Jill," he said. Her mouth was so full, she couldn't answer him. Instead, she made a little gesture with her hand and prayed silently that she didn't have spaghetti sauce all over her mouth. "I'd like to sit with you," Toby continued, "but I guess it wouldn't look too good. We're supposed to be opponents, after all."

Before she could answer, he disappeared to the other side of the cafeteria. Fate was cruel, Jill thought. It never let you run into a boy when you'd just brushed your hair or put on fresh lipstick. No. If there was a boy you liked and were interested in making a good impression on, fate would arrange things so you ran into him when your mouth was full of spaghetti.

She was still contemplating the cruelties of fate when Pam slid into the chair beside her. "Hi," Pam said cheerfully. "Did I miss anything?"

Jill shook her head. "Where's your lunch?" she asked.

Pam produced an apple and polished it on the front of her blouse. "Right here," she said.

"Is that all you're eating?" Jill asked. "No wonder you're so thin."

"Let's leave my body out of this," Pam said. "Besides, have I got news for you."

Jill pushed her lunch tray aside. If Pam could live on next to nothing, so could she. "What news?" she asked.

"I found out who Toby's campaign manager is," Pam told her.

Jill leaned forward eagerly. "Who?" she asked.

"You'll never guess," Pam said. "Not in a million years."

"I don't want to guess," Jill said impatiently. "I just want to know who's handling his campaign." She glanced over to where Toby was sitting, trying to spot his dark-gold head.

Pam's eyes opened like kaleidoscopes. "You like him, don't you?" she asked.

Jill felt her cheeks grow warm. She tried to make her voice sound casual. "Why shouldn't I?" she asked, remembering to use the politician's trick of answering a question with a question. "Doesn't everyone in Westmore like Toby Martin?"

Pam laughed. "I hope not," she said. "Otherwise you and I are doing a lot of work for nothing." She paused, and her voice turned serious again. "What I mean is," she said, "you like him a lot. You've got a crush on him."

Jill was about to deny it, but felt her cheeks turn from pink to red. Pam would never be fooled by such an obvious fib. Instead, Jill said, "If you breathe a word of it to anyone, I'll kill you."

"Heavens," Pam said, "a death threat! Don't worry. Wild horses couldn't drag it out of me."

"Good," Jill said, relieved. She knew she could count on Pam. Even if her friend actually were tied to a team of wild horses, she'd never betray Jill's secret. "Now," Jill continued, "tell me who his campaign manager is."

Pam glanced up. "She just walked in the door," she said.

Jill turned and looked toward the door of the cafeteria. "*Erica?*" she questioned. "*Erica Babcock?* You've got to be kidding!"

"It's true though," Pam said.

"And I thought Toby was *smart*," Jill said.

Pam shrugged and bit into the apple. "Maybe she made him an offer he couldn't refuse," she volunteered.

"Like what?" Jill asked. Pam rolled her eyes to indicate that the possibilities were limitless. Jill snorted with disgust. "You have a *ter*rible mind, you know that?"

"Only where Erica is concerned," Pam replied. "Look, I've got to go—told Tim I'd meet him at his locker before sixth period. Why don't I call you tonight and we can go over those questions then, okay?"

"Okay," Jill said. She watched as Erica made a beeline for Toby's table. How could someone as smart as Toby be taken in by someone like Erica? Jill wondered. Didn't he see that she was just managing his campaign in order to get close to him? Of course, there was always the possibility that he understood that perfectly well and simply didn't care. But Jill didn't want to believe that. Not about Toby.

She got up and carried her tray to the conveyor belt. She was headed out of the cafeteria when she felt a hand on her elbow.

"Hi, Jill," a voice said. "Mind if I walk with you? There's something I want to talk to you about."

Jill looked up. She'd known Nick Donnelly most of her life, but until now she hadn't realized how tall he'd grown. "Hi, Nick," she answered, falling into step with him. Three years ago, in the eighth grade, she'd had a terrific crush on Nick, but he hadn't even known she was alive. She guessed she'd forgiven him by now. "What's new?"

"I just wondered how your campaign was going," he said. He paused and added, "I mean, is there anything I can do to help?"

Jill glanced at him. Nick had sandy hair, a shade redder than her own, and clear green eyes. "Thanks for the offer, Nick," she said. "I'll let you know."

Nick looked disappointed. "I do exert some influence on the student council, you know," he said.

Jill laughed. "What are you going to do? Bribe the rest of the council to vote for me?"

"Toby did," Nick said.

"What?"

"Well, not Toby exactly—his campaign manager, Erica Babcock." Nick rolled his eyes to show how he felt about Erica. "She came to the council meeting last week and asked if any of us wanted to sign up to work on the campaign. Then later she just *happened* to mention that kids who worked on the campaign would be invited to this super party if Toby won. I'd call that bribery, wouldn't you?"

Jill shook her head. "I can't believe it," she said.

"I was there," Nick insisted. "I know what happened."

"Oh, I believe *you*, Nick, and I guess I believe that Erica—the little skunk—would pull something like that. I just don't believe that Toby knew what she was up to."

Nick wasn't so optimistic. "Whether he knew or not," he said, "he *should* know. It's his responsibility to."

They walked a few more yards in silence. Jill couldn't believe that Toby would let something like that happen. But Nick was right—he had a moral responsibility to know what was going on. She felt Nick's broad hand on her elbow. "So what do you say?" he asked.

"About what?"

"You know," he said. "Letting me get some support for you in the student council. I've got a few favors I could call in."

Jill found his green eyes fastened on her. There was more than political enthusiasm in them, and the thought flickered through Jill's mind that Nick might be interested in her. "I don't want to win that way, Nick," she told him. "Tell you what though—there's a campaign meeting the day after tomorrow after school. Why don't you come?"

Nick smiled. "I will," he said. "There must be something I can do to get you elected."

Two days later, at the campaign meeting, Nick made a point of sitting next to Jill. When the meeting broke up, he offered her a ride home. "I'm sorry, Nick," she told him, "I'm going over to Pam's house for a while."

"Oh," he said. "Well, next time, then."

"Sure," Jill said. "Next time."

Later that afternoon Pam looked at her with inquisitive dark eyes. "I didn't know that," she said, a smile playing around her mouth.

"Know what?" Jill asked.

"Know that Nick Donnelly has a crush on you."

Jill decided to use her politician's trick to evade the issue. "Does he?" she asked.

But Pam wasn't about to be put off. "You can see very well that he does. It's pretty obvious, isn't it?"

Jill didn't respond. Nick had a crush on her, she had a crush on Toby, *Erica* had a crush on Toby. She wondered who the voters had a crush on.

Jill decided against telling Pam about Erica's attempt to sway the student council votes. What would be the point? she wondered. It would only make Pam furious. And if Pam decided to fight Erica's fire with fire of her own, the whole election might get out of hand. Win or lose, Jill was determined to run an honest campaign.

The day before the big school assembly, when each of the candidates would give a speech and answer questions from the floor, Pam arrived at Jill's house shortly after dinner. The minute Jill saw her friend's face, she knew that something was wrong. Pam's dark eyes glowed with anger and her small compact body was tense with energy. "I can't *believe* what she's trying to do." Pam exploded as soon as the two girls were alone in Jill's room.

"What who's trying to do?" Jill questioned—as if she needed to ask. Somehow Jill knew that Erica was the source of Pam's fury.

"Erica, that's who," Pam retorted. "Do you know what she's saying?" Jill shook her head and Pam continued. "She's saying that you're *sure* you're going to win the election. *That's* why you aren't campaigning hard."

"But I *am* campaigning hard," Jill protested.

"Not as hard as she is." Pam snorted. She sat down beside Jill on the edge of the bed.

"Well," Jill said, "I guess it shouldn't surprise me. I mean, I've always known she didn't like me. I just didn't know how much."

Pam sighed. "It's a little more than your old rivalry, Jill," she said.

"What do you mean?"

"Don't you see?" Pam asked, brushing her short dark hair back behind her ears. "Erica's got a tremendous crush on Toby. She knows he asked you to be his campaign manager, and the only reason she got the job is because you turned it down. She's fighting you for more than an election, Jill—she's fighting you for Toby."

"But that's ridiculous," Jill said.

"Maybe," Pam admitted grudgingly, "but that's the way it is."

Jill bit her lip. For a split second she wished she'd never decided to run for class president. She wished she'd accepted Toby's offer to manage his campaign. If she'd done that, she wondered, what would have happened? Would she and Toby be in love, a couple? Suddenly Jill felt very lonely. She felt she'd given up something wonderful—and for what? For an election that was getting messier each and every day. Then she remembered why she decided to run in the first place—because she knew being president would make her senior year memorable and because in her heart she believed she was the best person for the job. "I don't want this campaign to get out of hand," she warned Pam. "No matter what Erica thinks—or *does*—I don't want to stoop to her level. I don't want things to get personal."

Pam was silent for a minute. Then she said, "Even so, Jill, we've got to do something—otherwise we'll lose the election. We've got to bring you to the voters' attention and put Erica's rumors to rest." She waited a moment and added, "Do you see now why I thought those posters were so important?"

Jill remembered the issue of the campaign posters. It had almost caused a fight between the two girls. Toby's father, it was rumored, had donated fifty dollars to his son's campaign fund. The money spent was evident in the form of elaborate professionally printed posters on the walls of Westmore High. Pam wanted Jill to come out with posters that were equally impressive.

"I don't have fifty dollars," Jill had protested.

"Well," Pam said, "we'll have to raise funds. If everyone on your staff contributes two or three dollars, we'll have enough."

But Jill had refused. "That's too much like buying the election," she said. "The point isn't to see who can spend more money than anyone else. The point is to see who can offer the voters the best representation."

Pam had rolled her eyes at the ceiling. "You're too much of an idealist to be in politics," she'd said.

Now Jill's idealism had backfired on her. She'd worked hard to run an honest campaign, devoid of gimmicks, bribes, and attention-getting stunts. Now Erica was turning that against her by saying Jill was so sure of victory, she didn't have to campaign. It was unfair, Jill thought, unfair! When she looked up, Pam was staring at her, arms folded across her chest.

"I don't know what you're smiling about," Pam admonished. "What are you going to do about all of this anyway?"

Jill thought for a minute. "Exactly what I was going to do before," she said. "I'm going to the assembly tomorrow and give the best speech I can."

Pam's mouth dropped open. "You mean, you aren't even going to try to stop Erica?" she asked. "You're going to let her get away with this?"

"If I make an issue of it," Jill said, "it will only give Erica more to go on, won't it? If we refuse to sink to her level—refuse to get involved in any sort of argument with her—she'll *have* to shut up. Otherwise she'll end up looking like an idiot."

"I'm not so sure," Pam said grimly.

"Even so," Jill said, "that's what I'm going to do. My Erica Policy, if you want to call it that. Are you on my side?"

"Of *course*, I am," Pam said. "I just want you to think about one thing. Would you bend this far backward if Toby weren't involved? If Erica were somebody else's campaign manager, would you be just as willing to play hands-off?"

Jill looked away from Pam's piercing eyes without answering. She wasn't evading the issue this time. Not at all. This time she honestly didn't know the answer herself.

They drew straws to determine their speaking order at the assembly. Kathy, with the shortest straw, was to speak first. Toby would go second and Jill last. As Jill sat on the stage beside Toby, listening to Kathy's speech, she tried to decide whether going last was lucky or not. She wouldn't have wanted to be first, of course. But going last meant she would follow Toby—Toby, who, sitting beside her, looked as calm as if he did this every day of his life. He didn't even have notes with him, Jill saw. Her own lap was full of three-by-five cards, and butterflies seemed to be fluttering in her stomach. By the time Toby was through speaking, she thought, she'd have forgotten everything she planned to say.

Kathy's speech ended, followed by polite, patient applause. Only six students stood up to ask her questions, and three of those questions had obviously been planned in advance by Kathy's campaign staff. She sat down before her allotted fifteen minutes were up, and Toby rose to take his turn at the podium.

From where Jill was sitting—behind the lectern and to the side of it—she had a three-quarter view of Toby. She saw him smile at the audience as if he were greeting each one of them personally even though, with the overhead stage lights on, it was impossible to see beyond the first row. Something happened to Toby when he started to speak, Jill noticed. Instead of becoming nervous and ill at ease, he became more charming than ever. The lights beamed down on his curly blond hair, sending golden glints in all directions. He gathered excitement as he spoke, and the conclusion of his speech was greeted with enthusiastic applause. He fielded so many questions from the floor that Mrs. Hanson, the teacher who had organized the assembly, had to interrupt him when his time was up.

I'll never be able to follow that, Jill thought as Toby took his seat. *Never in a million years*.

Toby sat down beside her. He was drenched with sweat, as if he'd just finished running a marathon, but he was smiling. "Good luck," he whispered to her as she stood up, and gave her elbow a friendly little squeeze.

Jill tried to smile back at him, but she was afraid her expression was more of a grimace. She felt like a condemned prisoner about to mount the steps to the guillotine. What if her mind went blank and she spent ten minutes simply staring at the audience? What if she was asked a question she couldn't answer? What if she lost control of herself in the middle of the speech and began laughing uncontrollably? The possibilities for disaster, she thought, were endless. She struggled to put them out of her head and began the speech she'd spent so much time rehearsing in front of her bedroom mirror.

The speech was timed to take exactly ten minutes. That left five minutes for questions from the floor. Jill glanced at her watch—2:15—when she began and again—2:22—as she finished. She'd hurried the speech in her nervousness, trimming it by three minutes. That didn't worry her particularly. She would just answer a few more questions than she'd planned to.

What *did* worry her was what happened when she finished speaking. There was almost no applause— not even the polite applause Kathy had received. Instead, there was an embarrassing trickle that must have come, Jill knew, from Pam and Tim and her campaign workers. She stood at the podium in shock. What was *wrong*? What had she said? The smattering of applause died away, and Jill stood in complete silence. She felt her cheeks grow hot with humiliation. Suddenly Mrs. Hanson rushed up to her. "Thank you, Jill," the teacher said brightly. "Now the floor is open for questions."

More silence. Jill shaded her eyes and looked out across the audience, but she failed to see a single hand.

I'm going to die, she thought. *Right here, right now. This is terrible—terrible!* Finally she saw a hand go up in the darkness. "Yes," she said.

"I was wondering, what do you think about making pep fest attendance optional instead of mandatory?"

Jill recognized Pam's voice at once. She was grateful that Pam had come to her rescue, and she took as long as possible to answer the question. She answered two more questions before she sat down—one question from Tim Sanderson and one from Nick Donnelly. She would have to remember—someday, when she could look him in the eye—to thank Nick for helping her out.

After what seemed an eternity of public humiliation, Jill took her seat again. Toby, embarrassed for her, didn't look up. Thank goodness for small favors, Jill thought. Toby's blue eyes would have pushed her right over the edge. There was no telling what she might have done.

Jill hurried backstage as soon as the assembly was over. Pam came rushing up to her. "What went wrong?" Jill asked. "What did I *say*?"

Pam's dark eyes burned with anger. "*You* didn't say anything," she said. "Someone said it for you." She handed Jill a sheet of paper that was obviously a Xerox copy. "This was distributed to everyone on the way into the assembly," she said.

Jill took the paper from Pam. In the upper left-hand corner was Jill's tenth-grade yearbook picture, poorly reproduced in black and white. Next to it, in quotes, was the sentence *Hi, I'm Jill Farrell*. Jill looked questioningly at Pam. "We didn't put this out, did we?" she asked.

"Of course not," Pam snapped. "Keep reading."

Jill read aloud.

"Hi, I'm Jill Farrell. I'd be lying if I didn't say I'm probably the most popular girl in Westmore High. Popularity is something I'm used to. I've been popular ever since I moved here nine years ago. I was your eighth-grade class president, the star of the ninth-grade spring play, and assistant junior editor on this year's school paper. So it makes sense that I should be senior class president, doesn't it? I mean, I have the *experience* for the job. My opponents are spending a lot of time and energy trying to get your votes. Well, they *need* to—they just don't have the kind of record I do. And I know that when it's time to choose the candidate you want to lead next year's senior class, you'll do what you've always done and VOTE FOR JILL FARRELL!"

Jill's hand was shaking. "I can't believe this," she said, crumpling the sheet into a ball. "This makes me look like the most obnoxious, most conceited person in the world."

"Exactly," Pam said.

Well, Jill thought, at least she knew why no one had applauded for her.

"Jill?"

Jill looked up into the friendly eyes of Nick Donnelly. He was holding a copy of the sheet in his hand. "I know you didn't put this out, Jill," he said. "But I'm afraid everyone *thinks* you did. Do you know who's behind it?"

Jill looked across the room to where Toby and Erica were standing. Toby's back was to her, but

Erica met her eye with a look of triumph. Jill stared at her a long moment before turning back to Nick. "I think I have a pretty good idea," she told him.

Nick didn't ask who the culprit was. Instead, he said, "Look, let's get out of here. I drove to school today—can I give you a ride home?"

This time Jill gratefully accepted Nick's offer. Nothing would be worse, she thought, than having to face a bus full of her classmates.

But she would have to face them sometime, she knew. And, more than that, she would have to decide what to do about what had happened today. She refused to believe that Toby had anything to do with it. This kind of stunt, she decided, had to be Erica's bright idea. In fact, if she knew Erica, Erica would do her best to fool Toby as she had fooled the rest of the class. But as much as she wanted to excuse Toby, she knew that he was, in a way, responsible. As Nick had pointed out before, Toby had an obligation to know what was going on, to know what kind of people were working for him.

There were two ways to handle the situation, Jill decided. She could go directly to Erica and confront her, or she could simply ignore the whole episode. Both plans had their pluses and minuses. On one hand Jill longed to make Erica admit what she had done. But wouldn't getting into an argument with Erica simply mean she'd be sinking to Erica's level? There was another factor to take into consideration, too, and that was simple fear. Erica, as Jill had already discovered, was capable of fighting dirty when the necessity arose. What would happen then, Jill wondered, if the two of them came face to face? Jill pictured the two of them locked in combat while their fellow classmates looked on. Not exactly a dignified image for a presidential candidate to present, she thought.

Perhaps the best way to handle the situation was simply to rise above it and look the other way. But that would let Erica off scot-free. Jill sighed. The more she thought about it, the more it seemed there was no right way to handle the situation. The *real* right way, she decided, would be to drop Erica into a vat of chocolate syrup and keep her there until the election was over. *That* would be extremely satisfying. Jill smiled to herself as she thought of the sticky syrup coating Erica's long white-blond hair. Too bad it wasn't a real possibility.

♡

If you think Jill decides to confront Erica, go to page 82.

If you think Jill decides to keep quiet, go to page 97.

Jill's hand paused between each number she dialed. Asking Dennis to Toby's victory party had seemed like such a good idea when she'd talked it over with Pam. Now she wasn't so sure. Picking up the phone and calling him was turning out to be a lot more difficult than she'd imagined. What if he was too busy to come? What if he didn't even remember who she was? Maybe she should give up the whole idea and go to Toby's party alone.

But it was too late. Her finger had dialed the last digit and the phone was ringing.

"Hello." It was a woman's voice. *Good,* Jill thought. *Maybe I dialed the wrong number.*

"Is Dennis Rhodes there?"

"Just a second, I'll get him."

Jill's fingers tightened on the telephone receiver while she waited. Her heart made its way from her chest up into her throat. She hoped her voice wouldn't come out in a high-pitched squeal.

"Hello?"

"Dennis? Hi, this is Jill—Jill Farrell."

"Jill! This is great—I was just thinking about you."

Relief. There was a God in heaven after all. Jill tried to make her voice sound casual. "Yeah? Really? I guess we must be telepathic."

Dennis laughed. Jill pictured him throwing his dark head back a little, the way he had on the day of the picnic. "I was hoping for more than a meeting of minds," he said, chuckling.

The conversation was easier than Jill had imagined.

They talked about what they'd done during the week and about their classes. Still, when it was time to ask him to the party, her heart started skipping around in her chest again. "The party's going to be a lot of fun," she told him. "But it'll be a lot *more* fun if you come with me."

There was a pause on the other end of the line. Jill felt a sinking sensation in her stomach. "Gee, Jill," Dennis said, "I'd really like to go, but—" Oh, no, she thought, he was going to turn her down. Jill wondered if anyone had ever died during a telephone conversation. Probably not. She'd be the first in history. "There's a night game that night," Dennis continued. "In fact, I was going to ask you if you wanted to come to it."

Suddenly things looked brighter. At least he *wanted* to go out with her. "That's too bad," Jill said buoyantly.

But Dennis was sincerely disappointed. "I really wanted to get together with you," he said. "Hey, wait. I've got an idea. The game should be over around nine thirty. I could shower and drive straight into Westmore. Could I meet you at the party?"

"That'd be perfect," Jill said. "Let me give you the address."

A few minutes later, when she hung up the telephone, Jill smiled to herself. A piece of cake, she thought with an air of satisfaction. Nothing to it. Asking a boy out was the easiest thing in the world. She picked up the phone again and dialed Pam's number, eager to tell her all about it.

Jill checked her reflection in the mirror one last time. She was wearing her favorite shirt—a plaid madras with metallic gold thread woven through it—and blue jeans that could still be considered new. Her hair fell around her shoulders in a smooth flip and her makeup, for once, was just right. She hoped it would all last until Dennis showed up at the party. Tucking her keys, a little money, and a tube of pale pink lip gloss into the back pocket of her jeans, she stepped to the top of the stairs.

"I'm ready to go, Dad," she called.

"Okay, honey," her father's voice rang back.

By the time she got downstairs, her father was standing by the door, car keys in hand. Mr. Farrell was a tall man with thick black hair and blue eyes. Jill often thought how unfair it was that neither she nor Penny had inherited his coloring. "Thanks for giving me a ride, Dad," she said. "I appreciate it."

"Anytime, honey. You sure you won't need one home too?"

Jill shook her head. "Dennis is meeting me at the party. Don't worry—he won't stand me up." Why, she wondered, did parents always expect the worst? Just habit, she decided.

"Just remember," her father said a few minutes later when he dropped her off in front of the Martin home, "in case you *do* need a ride, your mother and I will be home all evening."

Jill nodded and waved good-bye. Then she mounted the steps and rang the doorbell. A waterfall of chimes echoed inside the house. Jill looked up at the impressive, two-story home. It was lovely but formal, and a little out of place among the casual ranch houses that surrounded it. In a way it was like Toby himself—it looked very much as if it were trying to get somewhere else, as if it were trying to escape its down-to-earth neighbors. Mrs. Martin answered the door and pointed Jill toward the large family room at the back of the house.

Toby stood at the door of the room greeting his guests. He was wearing a spotless white shirt and dark trousers. He could have been a junior congressman greeting his constituents, Jill thought, or a movie star. "Jill," he said, flashing her a smile so irresistible that, for a minute, she regretted having asked Dennis to the party. "Gosh, you look wonderful."

Jill glowed. She would have liked to talk to Toby longer, but more guests were crowding behind her. She moved into the room, which was already beginning to become crowded. Along a wall a table was loaded with soft drinks and food—guacamole dip, black bean dip, and a dip that, when Jill tasted it, turned out to be jalapeño. The hot pepper dip left her mouth tingling, and she reached for a soda.

"Pretty hot stuff, huh?" a friendly voice said.

"It sure is," Jill said, sipping her soda. The voice belonged to Caz Willard, whom she'd known since he moved to Westmore the year after she did. "How are things going, Caz?"

"Fine," Caz answered. "Good, in fact. Of course, like everyone else, I can't wait for school to let out. I've got a great summer job lined up."

Jill smiled at him. He was a nice boy, the kind of boy she'd want to have for a brother. "That's great, Caz," she said.

Caz nodded and dusted corn chip crumbs off his hands. Someone had put a tape on Toby's portable player and turned the volume up. Couples were already moving toward the bare center of the room. "Want to dance?" Caz asked.

Jill looked for a place to set her soda down. "Sure," she said.

Dancing with Caz was nice. The whole party, in fact, was nice. Still, Jill was eager for Dennis to arrive. That, she thought, would make the evening more than just nice.

When she and Caz finished dancing, Jill drifted back to the table where she'd left her soda. "*There* you are," Toby's voice sounded behind her. "I've been looking all over for you."

Jill turned around. Even now, now when she'd entirely given up the idea of having a relationship with him, Toby could produce an amazing effect on her. She smiled and waited for him to continue. Toby reached out and took her hand. "Come on," he said, "there's someone I want you to meet."

"Who?" Jill teased. "Your chief campaign contributor? Your running mate when you make your move on the White House?"

Toby shook his head. "Uh-uh," he said. "My girlfriend."

The words ran through Jill like a knife through soft butter. His girlfriend! He had never mentioned seeing someone. In fact, Jill thought, he had seemed to go out of his way to create the illusion that he was totally unattached. Of course, she remembered, there *was* that phone call he'd received at her house. Still, she was surprised to learn that Toby was seeing someone often enough to consider her—whoever she was—his girlfriend. Jill drew in her breath. Thank goodness she had given up the idea of trying to start a relationship with Toby. She had narrowly—just narrowly—missed making an utter fool of herself.

Whoever she is, Jill thought, looking around the room, she must be fabulous. She must be stunning if she's going out with Toby.

Toby lead her all the way across the room. A small, plain-looking girl was standing with her hands at her sides, as if she were waiting for something to do. "Jill," Toby said, drawing her up to the girl, "this is Mary Gardner. You probably don't know her—she goes to Saint Catherine's."

"Hi," Jill said, extending her hand.

"Hello," Mary said, smiling at Jill.

Jill couldn't believe that this was Toby's girlfriend. She had expected someone stunningly, maddeningly gorgeous. This girl, she noticed, wasn't even wearing lipstick. Mary continued to smile and stare at Jill with sweet, cocker spaniel–like brown eyes. Jill had no idea what to say to her, and looked at Toby for help. Toby, however, had disappeared to take care of his guests.

"Toby told me how hard you worked on his campaign," Mary volunteered at last.

"Oh," Jill said, "not that hard, really. I'm glad he won though. It would have been terrible to have done it all for nothing."

Mary smiled again. She must have a terrific mind, Jill thought. That must be what Toby sees in her— leave it to Toby to go for a superbrain. "Have you had class elections at Saint Catherine's yet?" Jill asked. "You could run for president too. Then you and Toby would be a two-president couple."

Mary laughed softly. "Oh, I'm not the type for that," she said. "Toby's the type to be president and things like that."

For the next five minutes, Mary talked about
Toby—how handsome he was, how smart he was,
how certain it was that he would be a very successful
man someday. In the whole five minutes Mary didn't
say a single thing about herself. Her essential interest in life, Jill concluded, was Toby Martin. No
wonder Toby liked her, Jill thought—she was a one-
woman fan club. Realizing that somehow made Toby
seem a lot less enchanting.

Jill was still thinking about Mary Gardner when
she felt a hand on her elbow. "I guess I'm in the right
place," the voice belonging to the hand said.

Jill turned around and found herself looking at
Dennis. He was wearing a dark green western shirt
with white piping on it. He looked even cuter than
she remembered. "You're in the *per*fect place," she
answered. "How was the game?"

"We lost, five–seven, but I knocked in two runs."

"That's great," Jill said. "You deserve a reward.
How about a soda?"

He winked at her. "No root beer showers?" he
asked.

"Nope," she said. "I promise."

Dennis pulled the tab back on a can of soda and
took a long sip. He looked around the room, then
back at Jill. "It looks like a good party," he said.

"It is," she answered, and added, "I've been learning a lot." She was thinking about Toby Martin and
Mary Gardner.

Dennis's dark straight eyebrows drew together.
"Learning? What about?"

Jill shrugged. "I guess you could put it under the
general heading of life."

"Uh-oh," Dennis said. "Sounds serious."

Jill laughed. "It isn't—not at all. Come on, let's dance."

They mingled with the other couples on the floor. Suddenly Jill felt a rush of pleasure. The party, which had been just nice until Dennis arrived, was suddenly special and exciting. She imagined that people were looking at her and wondering who the cute stranger with the dark hair was that she was dancing with. It would be just fine with her, she decided, if the party went on all night.

It didn't of course. In fact, Jill and Dennis decided to leave a half hour before the party actually ended. They were finishing the last of the guacamole when Dennis asked her what time she had to be home. "Twelve thirty," Jill said, "but . . ." she hesitated.

"But what?" Dennis asked.

"Well, my parents go to bed around midnight. I know it's kind of a drag, but I'd sort of like you to meet them. I mean, they absolutely *insist* on meeting everybody I go out with, so if you want to go out with me again, I'm afraid you'll have to meet them sometime." Suddenly she felt nervous. What if he never *wanted* to see her again? She stabbed a fragment of corn chip into the dip. "Of course, if you don't want to go out with me again, it's another matter completely, so—"

Dennis reached out and took her hand, corn chip and all. "I think I'd better meet your parents," he said seriously. "Let's go."

As they walked down the driveway and out into the street where his car was parked, Dennis slipped his arm around her shoulders. Jill put her arm around his waist and settled her stride to his gait. "I'm really sorry we had to leave early," she murmured.

"Shhh," Dennis said. Very quickly and very softly, he kissed her—first on the cheek, then on the mouth. He was taller than she was, and Jill had to tip her head back a little. She saw that, overhead, all the stars in the universe were shining down on them.

That was the beginning of their relationship. The next weekend, Jill and Dennis and Pam and Tim drove into Fort Worth to see *Return of the Jedi*. Jill didn't care for the movie all that much—she had liked *E.T.* much more—but she loved sitting next to Dennis in the dark movie theater, her hand bumping his when she reached into the cardboard box for kernels of popcorn.

They started calling each other every day after that. In the middle of the week Dennis drove into Westmore on the pretext of returning the sweater Jill had left in his car. The following Saturday Jill borrowed her mother's car and made the trip to Alta Vista to see Dennis in a home game. When prom time arrived, they decided to go to the dances at both schools.

"Jill's going steady. Jill's going steady," Penny sang out, leaning over the banister and looking down at Jill in her pastel blue prom dress.

Jill glanced up at her sister. Penny's long, lank hair was trailing down over the banister like a flag. Jill would have liked nothing better than to reach up, grab a handful, and pull as hard as she could. But she restrained herself. She was all dressed up, and Dennis was due any minute. "Why don't you grow up?" she asked, hoping she sounded aloof and sophisticated.

Penny made a face and retreated up the stairs, her singsong chorus of "Jill's going steady," echoing behind her.

Jill sighed. It was useless to argue with Penny—especially when Penny was right. She and Dennis *were* going steady. They'd never said it in so many words, but neither of them dated anyone else and neither of them wanted to. Wasn't that what going steady was? Jill smiled at the realization. She had never thought about it directly before—about her relationship with Dennis. Now it seemed that, without even trying, she had found the special person she'd been looking for for so long.

"You look like you're about to launch yourself into orbit," her father said, coming up behind her and hugging her. He held his camera in one hand and was waiting for Dennis to come so he could take their picture.

Jill smiled at him and pulled away so her dress wouldn't get crumpled. Taffeta, she'd discovered, creased the minute you breathed on it. "I'm not going to launch myself into orbit," she said. "I'm going to stand right here and wait for Dennis."

"Well," her father said, "you look terrific just *standing* there."

"The inner glow of happiness, I guess," Jill said. She'd wanted to say *love*—the inner glow of love. Somehow she couldn't. She guessed it didn't matter. Love and happiness were much the same.

When Dennis arrived, her mother came out into the foyer and watched while Mr. Farrell snapped pictures of them. "Get a few in the living room by the piano," Mrs. Farrell said, and her husband repositioned them and took another half-dozen shots.

"I'm glad that's over," Jill said when they finally left the house.

Dennis laughed. "Brace yourself. It'll be the same thing all over again at my house *next* weekend."

Jill took his hand. "I won't mind," she said. "Not as long as you're there with me."

"I will be," Dennis said, and hugged her.

They never could decide which of the two proms had been more fun. Both were wonderful. The whole spring, in fact, was wonderful. Every day since they had met had been special and wonderful. Jill sometimes wondered if life on earth could possibly be any better than this. She always came to the conclusion that it couldn't be. Everything was perfect just as it was. She and Dennis were happy together, and she had the additional happiness of knowing that her friends and her family liked Dennis too. Her father, who had remained a Houston Astros fan even after the family moved to Westmore, often coaxed Dennis into watching a few innings of a ball game on television with him while Jill waited patiently—and sometimes *im*patiently—for their date to begin. And her mother, Jill knew, liked Dennis as much as her father did. If she hadn't, she wouldn't have been so liberal about letting Jill use her car to drive to Alta Vista. She would have, Jill knew, made transportation an obstacle to keep them apart. As it was, Jill had almost free use of the little blue Omni.

"That road between Westmore and Alta Vista must be getting pretty threadbare," her father would tease as Jill left the house. "Drive carefully."

Jill did drive carefully. Always. Even on days like

today when she was running late. Today had been a hectic one from the beginning, when she'd had to stop and sew a button on her blouse before she could leave for school. Then she'd spent her entire lunch period working with Lisa Valdez on the final school newspaper of the year. To top things off her favorite teacher had dropped a bombshell on her. It turned out to be a happy bombshell, but it was a bombshell nonetheless.

Mrs. Ingersoll, her English teacher, announced that there would be no final exam for the class. As soon as the wild cheers had died down, she announced the alternative: a writing assignment, no more than ten typed pages, of the student's choice. Jill received the news with mixed feelings. She loved writing, and knew that, in the long run, a writing assignment would teach her a lot more than an hour-long test would. On the other hand there was the time factor. She would put so many more hours of effort into the writing assignment than she would into studying for a test—and at this point in her life Jill felt she didn't have all that many hours to spare. Going steady, she was discovering, was a very time-consuming operation.

Even so, Jill felt excited about the assignment. She already had an idea for a short story. She stayed after school to work on it and was late getting home, late changing clothes, and late picking Pam up. She hoped they weren't going to be late to the baseball game. It was, as she knew very well, a very special game. The regular season had ended, and the ten teams in the Eastern Star conference were starting round-robin play-offs for the conference title. This afternoon Alta Vista was playing Westmore at Alta Vista.

"Tim's so nervous about this, he couldn't even eat lunch today," Pam said as they drove the ribbon of double-lane highway that connected the two towns. "I mean, if Westmore gets eliminated in the first round, it'll be just awful."

Jill nodded and kept her eyes on the road. It'd be just as awful—for Dennis anyway—if Alta Vista got eliminated. She glanced quickly over at Pam. "It's too bad," she said, "that one of us has *got* to lose."

Pam laughed, a nervous, anxious laugh. "Look on the bright side," she said. "One of us has *got* to win."

They sat side by side at the game, rooting spiritedly for the opposing teams. In the seventh inning the game was tied, and Westmore was at bat with a man on third and two outs. A base hit would score the go-ahead run. With a count of one ball and one strike, the batter hit a long fly that looked as if it might go over the right-field fence. It didn't though—there wasn't enough wind to carry it. Dennis, playing right field, looked up, ready to position himself under the ball. Watching him, Jill knew he'd lost the ball in the sun. *Oh, Lord*, she thought, *he's going to miss it. The run's going to score.* She drew in a deep breath and jumped to her feet. "Your right!" she screamed as loud as she could. Dennis shifted his position, spotted the ball, and got his glove under it just in time.

Jill sat back down. She'd screamed so loud, her throat hurt. Pam was glaring at her. Suddenly she realized what she'd done—robbed her own school of the go-ahead run. "Sorry, Pam," she said.

Pam looked at her a long minute. Then her dark eyes softened. "I would have done the same thing," she said.

Alta Vista scored twice in the next inning and hung on to win the game. Having defeated Westmore, their toughest opponent, Dennis felt his team had a good shot at the conference title. "We'll win," he said confidently. "Just as long as you're there to spot fly balls for me," he added, slipping his arm around Jill's waist and drawing her to him.

"I will be," Jill said. "I promise."

Jill had to cancel two dates with Dennis to get her English story done on time. She didn't regret it though—working on the story was wonderful. It rekindled her old childhood dream of growing up and being a famous writer. If she wanted that dream, she thought, she'd better get going—she was almost grown up.

Dennis called her every evening to ask how things were going. She told him about the problems she was having with her characters and how one scene just wouldn't come out right. She wouldn't read him any part of the story itself though. Somehow that didn't seem right. Instead, she told him he could read the whole thing when it was finished. Then she changed the subject and asked him how *his* classes were going. He told her about them, but mostly he wanted to talk about baseball. Alta Vista had defeated Maple Plain the week after they defeated Westmore, and the whole team was on a roll. School let out the Tuesday after Memorial Day, and everyone was living for June fifteenth, the day of the final play-off game. "We're going to be in it," Dennis would say, nervous and confident at the same time. "I *know* we're going to make it to that game."

Jill knew he'd be there too. She drew a big red

circle around June fifteenth on her calendar and decided to postpone looking for a summer job until the day had passed.

In all the excitement she almost forgot that her own school year was almost over. Three days before the last day of classes Mrs. Ingersoll handed back their writing assignments. Jill got an A + —for concept and execution—over an A - —for spelling and punctuation. She also got a personal note on the last page of her story: *Please see me after class.*

Jill waited impatiently for the bell to ring and for the rest of the students to leave the classroom. Then she went up to Mrs. Ingersoll's desk.

"Sit down, won't you, Jill?" the teacher said, crossing the room and closing the door. "Don't worry—I'll write you a pass for your next class. I want to talk to you about something."

Jill sat down on the edge of a desk top. The hum of passing students died away in the hall, and the bell for the next class rang. It seemed strange to be sitting here, in the empty room, instead of in chemistry. Maybe that was why she felt a strange sense of excitement.

Mrs. Ingersoll looked at her. "Have you ever heard of the Red River Conference?" the teacher asked.

Jill shook her head. She wondered if it were a division of high school teams, like the Eastern Star conference. "It's a writers' conference that's held every year," Mrs. Ingersoll continued, "just outside of Sherman, near the Red River. It's usually open to college students and older. I went there a few years ago, as a student, and loved it. I've been invited back this year as an instructor."

"That's wonderful," Jill said. "Congratulations."

Mrs. Ingersoll smiled. "Thanks. But the reason I wanted to talk to you was about you going, as a student. I'm sure I could get the age requirement waived. Your story was so good, Jill—I just think this would be a wonderful opportunity for you."

Jill's heart jumped. She hadn't expected anything like this. But as soon as she started to think about the idea, a thousand obstacles came up. How much would it cost? How long would she be away? Were her parents going to approve?

"It's a very wholesome environment," Mrs. Ingersoll assured her. "I think we can convince your parents of that. It lasts a week, and you can ride both ways with me, so transportation won't be a problem. The biggest expenses are the cost of the conference itself and room and board for a week. Of course, if you'd be willing to be my roommate, you could cut the last part of that in half."

Jill saw the obstacles falling away as quickly as they had appeared. She didn't know what the total cost would come out to be, but she had some money saved from baby-sitting. Besides, when her parents heard about it, they'd probably be willing to contribute to the expenses. Jill beamed. Just wait until she told Dennis. "That's great, Mrs. Ingersoll. I'd love to go—I'd really love to."

"Good. Here's a brochure explaining everything. Why don't you talk it over with your parents and let me know what they think?"

Jill walked down to hall to her next class, reading the brochure aloud as she walked. **Tenth Annual Red River Conference,** it said in boldface script. **June twelfth to June eighteenth.** *June twelfth to eighteenth!* Oh, no—she'd miss the final play-off games. After she'd promised Dennis she'd be there, she'd miss the final game of the year. The idea of missing the writers' conference, which she hadn't even known existed until fifteen minutes ago, was unbearable. She had to go, she just *had* to. On the other hand, what would happen if she missed the final play-off game? The thought worried her. Maybe missing the game—the one she'd promised to be there for—would change things between her and Dennis. Maybe their relationship would never be the same again.

Jill's mind searched for alternate solutions. She could attend the conference next year, of course. But next year wouldn't be the same. Next year, Mrs. Ingersoll wouldn't be there. And next year she wouldn't be a privileged, gifted writer who'd had the age requirement waived. Next year she'd just be an ordinary person. No, she wanted to go *this* year.

She felt hot tears working behind her eyes like cactus needles. She went into a rest room, turned on the faucet, and splashed cold water on her face. She stared at herself in the mirror. What had happened? This morning she had been splendidly, perfectly happy. Now she was confused. She had the uncomfortable, misery-provoking feeling of wanting two things when she could only have one. *If I ask Dennis,* she thought, *what will he tell me to do?* But she knew Dennis well enough to know that he wouldn't tell her to "do" anything. He would tell her to make up her own mind. And that, Jill knew, was exactly what she was going to have to do—make up her own mind.

♡

If you think Jill decides to go to the writers' conference, go to page 110.

If you think Jill decides to stay home, go to page 121.

Jill looked at her reflection in the full-length mirror that hung on the door of her bedroom closet. Thanks to a hefty advance on several allowances, she was wearing a new dress. It wasn't the pink-and-gray striped sweat shirt dress she'd seen in Minty's with Pam—when she had tried that one on, the pink stripes had looked terrible with her roan-colored hair. Instead, she'd found a dress in deep, soft gold that made her hair and skin glow. The dress had a dropped waist and a short, ruffled skirt. Best of all, it had a halter back, which set off her smooth tan shoulders to perfection.

Jill smiled at her reflection. It wasn't that she was conceited—she'd never been that. It's just that she was honest enough to know when she knew she looked good. And tonight, with peach blusher on her cheeks and a dusting of gold eye shadow on her lids, she knew she looked very good indeed—even if it had cost her a small fortune to get that way. She just hoped Toby would appreciate it. Because if he didn't, there wasn't going to be anyone else around who did. She had decided against inviting Dennis to the victory party, and she wasn't sure who else was going to be there.

On the way out of the house she kissed both of her parents good-bye. "Thanks for lending me the car, Dad," she said, picking up the keys.

"Anytime, honey," Mr. Farrell said, although "anytime" was hardly the philosophy that prevailed.

"Just be sure to drive carefully, and have a good time."

"I will," Jill promised. "Good night. Good night, Penny."

"Night," Penny answered, scarcely taking her eyes off *Dallas* on the TV screen.

There were lots of kids already at Toby's party by the time Jill arrived. This was the first time Jill had ever seen his entire campaign staff assembled in one place. No wonder he won, she thought, looking around. He got half the school to work for him.

She felt a warm arm around her bare shoulders and inhaled the familiar drift of after-shave. "Wow," Toby said, kissing her on the cheek and then holding her at arm's length to look at her. "Look what we've got here—the golden goddess. You look super, Jill. Just terrific!"

Jill felt herself blush with pleasure. "Thanks, Toby," she said. She let her eyes settle on him. The sun, she noticed, had brought out streaks of gold in his dark blond hair. "You look nice yourself."

Toby grinned at her. "I guess we make a pretty good couple, then, don't we?" he said. He slipped his arm around her waist and lowered his voice. "Excuse me a minute, will you? I've got to go take care of the worker bees."

Jill watched him glide off to another group of students, smiling at them and thanking them for the work they'd done. *I guess we make a pretty good couple, then, don't we?* Toby's words echoed in her mind. Did that mean he felt the same way about her that she felt about him? Did he mean that, as soon as the excitement of the election died down, he wanted to start a *real* relationship with her? He must, Jill decided. Why else would he have said a thing like that?

Full of confidence, she watched Toby talking to the group of kids. As soon as he was finished thanking them, she knew, he would return to her. They would glide through the party together, a golden king and queen, destined to rule. The thought was so delicious, she could hardly stand it.

Jill saw Toby turn away from the group. Her body, as if remembering the warmth of his arm around her, quickened its pulse. But instead of returning to her, he moved on to another group. Jill stifled her disappointment as she watched him. He can't help it, she assured herself. He has to pay attention to them. They worked on his election, after all. It was hard to keep watching Toby—hard to see him smiling at other girls the way he'd smiled at her, hard to see him give them quick, enthusiastic hugs. Finally Jill walked over to the large table that held the refreshments. Typical of Toby, the usual plastic cups and big two-liter bottles of soda were missing. So were the casual bowls of chips or popcorn. Instead, there was a glass punch bowl and, arranged on a plate beside it, bits of raw vegetables meant to be dipped into a sour cream–and–chives dip.

Jill filled a cup with punch and nibbled a piece of raw broccoli. She didn't want to risk dripping sour cream onto her new dress, but without the sour cream, she thought, the broccoli was pretty tasteless. She'd take chips any day.

"Oh, fantastic!" a voice beside her said. "*Crudités!*"

Jill turned just in time to see Erica Babcock digging a trough through the sour cream with a carrot spear. "Erica!" Jill said in surprise. "I didn't expect to see *you* here."

Erica glared at her. "Why not?" she asked, her sharp white teeth crunching down on the innocent carrot. She chewed for a minute, then swallowed, never taking her eyes off Jill. "I was invited, you know. I worked on Toby's campaign too."

This was news to Jill. "You did?" she asked.

"Of course," Erica said confidently. "He needed me—he told me so. I know everyone's still laughing at me for that note Hawks read out loud, but Toby likes me—*really* likes me. I can tell. And as soon as this election thing's all over, as soon as he has time, I'm sure he's going to ask me out."

"Oh, but, Erica—" Jill began, and stopped. Erica's words sounded foolish, but weren't they the same thoughts she'd been having herself? Hadn't she, too, until just now, been convinced that Toby intended to have a serious relationship with her? Swallowing the last dry piece of broccoli, Jill looked around the room with fresh eyes. "Erica," she said, "how many girls would you say there are for every boy at this party?"

Erica was many things, and far from stupid was one of them. She made a quick study of the room. "About five to one," she replied.

"Do you see what Toby's done?" Jill asked. "He's charmed us—*all* of us—into working for him."

"I don't believe you," Erica said. "You're just saying that because you hate me."

Jill sighed. In some ways Erica was about as mature as her sister, Penny. "I *don't* hate you," Jill said. "I never have. Besides, why would I tell you this if it weren't true? Believe me, I don't enjoy it any more than you do. Toby did the same thing to me. Until about two minutes ago I was convinced that he and I would end up getting married."

Erica looked at her. "Really?"

Jill nodded. "Really. I can't believe I was such an idiot."

Erica started to giggle. "Me either," she said. Jill wasn't sure how she meant this, but she let it pass. "Look," Erica said, nudging Jill in the ribs, "I guess we aren't the only suckers."

Jill followed Erica's glance. Vickie Olmstead and Sue Matthews were standing at the edge of the room directly across from them. Both girls were staring at Toby as if he were the president of the United States, instead of president-elect of next year's senior class. "This is weird," Jill said. "Like *Night of the Living Dead* or something. He's turned us all into absolute zombies."

Erica laughed again. This time, there was no trace of meanness in her voice when she spoke. "You're right, Jill. I never thought I'd agree with you about *any*thing, but you certainly seem to be right about Toby."

Jill began looking around for her purse. "This is too morbid for me," she said. "I'm leaving."

"Me too," Erica said. "Oh, gosh—I just remembered. I can't."

"Why not?" Jill asked.

Erica's face reddened. "I asked my mom to drop me off here. I didn't worry about a ride home because I was sure Toby would give me one."

"Come on, then," Jill said. "You can ride with me."

"Well—" Erica said hesitantly.

"Oh, come on, Erica. What do you think I'm going to do to you anyway? Crash the car into a tree just to

put an end to the Jill Farrell–Erica Babcock rivalry?
I'm not crazy, you know."

Erica laughed. "Okay. Thanks, Jill."

Toby caught up with them when they were almost
at the door. "You're not leaving, are you?" he asked,
his blue eyes looking crestfallen.

"Yes," Jill said. "It was a fascinating party though,
Toby. Thanks for inviting me."

"Me too," Erica said.

Jill looked at Toby. What would he do now? she
wondered. How would he manage both of them at
once? But Toby, who no doubt had a good deal of
practice at handling such situations, wasn't in the least
disturbed. He glided between them and put an arm
around the waist of each. "I refuse to let you go—I need
you here with me," he said in such a way that either
girl might think the remark was meant for her alone.

It was Jill who pulled herself away first. "We really
do have to go, Toby," she insisted.

"She's right," Erica said. "We're leaving."

"Well, good night, then," Toby said, looking at
them helplessly. It was like abandoning a child, Jill
thought—or a puppy.

Jill unlocked the car and got behind the wheel.
She leaned across the front seat to open Erica's door
for her.

"He's incredible," Jill said, starting the car and
glancing over her shoulder for traffic. "Just incredible!"

Erica laughed softly in the darkness. "You know,
Jill," she said, "maybe we're not as different as I
always thought we were."

On Saturday, the day after Toby's party, Jill went
over to Pam's house. Pam's mother was the junior

high school French teacher, and for that reason she was the only person in Westmore—in all of Texas probably, Jill thought—who subscribed to the Paris edition of *Vogue* magazine. Between comments on the improbability of French fashion, Jill told Pam everything that had happened the night before.

"I never did think Toby was the man for you," Pam said when Jill finished her story.

"Thanks," Jill said, turning a page of the magazine.

"For what?" Pam questioned.

"For not saying 'I told you so.' You'd have every right, you know."

Pam grinned. "I know," she said. She pointed to an emaciated model in an especially skimpy swimsuit, her skin glistening with what was supposed to be saltwater but in real life, Pam suggested, was probably a spraying of baby oil. "Wow, can you believe that? I'd feel naked—absolutely naked!"

Jill nodded. "I certainly wouldn't trust it not to peel off in the water."

"What do you want to bet though," Pam said, "that we see the marvelous Miss Babcock in something just like it this summer? It's exactly the kind of thing she'd go in for."

The two girls were lying on their stomachs on the floor of Pam's bedroom. Jill rolled over on her back, away from the magazine, and stretched. "Oh, come on, Pam," she said. "Erica's not that bad—not really. And after last night I'm not even sure she hates me anymore."

Pam looked at her and shook her head. "Are you kidding? You mean you actually think Erica's going to change? Jill, my sweet, you're living in a fool's paradise."

Jill laughed. "Maybe," she said, "but I can hope, can't I? I mean, that way at least something good would have come out of that party."

"Something good *did* come out of it," Pam told her.

"Like what, I'd like to know."

"Like you getting Toby Martin out of your head once and for all. Now you can concentrate on that cute ballplayer from Alta Vista. Are you still going to call him?"

Jill let out a glum sigh. "I'd like to, but I don't have any reason to now. I mean, before there was Toby's party to ask him to. Now I don't have any excuse."

"So?" Pam asked, her dark eyebrows arching above her dark eyes. "As my aunt in New York would say, 'So who needs an excuse?'" Pam shrugged her shoulders, perfectly mimicking the aunt who had come to visit two years ago.

Jill sat up. "*I* need an excuse, that's who."

"Why?"

"*Why?* Because if I just call him up and ask him out just because I'm *interested* in him . . . gosh, what if he turns me down?"

Pam rolled her eyes. "It's a good thing you weren't born a boy," she said. "You'd never have a date in your life. Look, Jill, this is serious. Romance and fun and all that stuff. Take a chance."

"That's easy for you to say," Jill protested.

"I've done it," Pam said.

"Oh, yeah? When?"

"Who do you think asked Tim out first?" Pam asked.

Jill's blue eyes fixed on Pam. "Is that true?" she questioned. "You never told me that before."

"I figure how Tim and I got together is no one's business but our own. The point is, it worked."

"Hmmm," Jill said. She still wasn't convinced that Pam was telling the truth. It wouldn't be unlike Pam to stretch a point for the sake of example.

"Well," Pam said at last, "are you going to call him?"

"I'm going to *think* about calling him," Jill said.

Pam pretended to threaten her with the heavy copy of Paris *Vogue*. "You're impossible," she yelled. "Impossible! If you never have another date, it'll be your own fault."

Jill was still thinking about what to do when she got home. "There was a phone call for you, honey," her mother said. "He wanted you to call back—number's by the telephone."

"He?" Jill questioned. She hoped it wasn't Toby—she wasn't up to handling him just now. After he'd won his election, she hoped he'd forgotten all about her.

But the name written on the notepad wasn't Toby's—it was Dennis Rhodes's. *This is perfect,* Jill thought. *My whole problem is solved.* Then, a second, sneakier thought came to her. *This way, I can tell Pam I came straight home and called Dennis.* Technically it was true. And if there was more to the story than that, it was, as Pam herself would say, nobody else's business.

"Dennis?" she said when a masculine voice sounded on the other end of the phone.

"Speaking," he answered. "Is this Jill?"

"Yeah. How are you?"

"I'm fine," he said.

That was how their conversation went for a while—just the ordinary stuff, nothing very exciting. But then, just when Jill was beginning to wonder why he'd called her, Dennis asked if she was free the following afternoon. "We've got a terrific municipal pool over here in Alta Vista," he said. "I thought maybe I could come over to Westmore, pick you up, and bring you back here for a while. Even if you don't like to swim, there's a great sundeck."

"I like to swim," Jill assured him. "I love to swim, in fact."

She could hear the pleasure in Dennis's voice when he said, "Really? That's terrific. And there's a place in town we can go afterward where they have this super barbecue."

"That sounds terrific," Jill said. "What time will you be here?"

"About noon? How does that sound?"

"Perfect," Jill said. "That'll give me time to change from church. Just one more question," she added playfully. "What do we do if it rains?"

Dennis's deep chuckle filled her ear. "Swimming is Plan A," he said. "If it rains, we'll have to go to Plan B."

They didn't have to go to Plan B though; not that day. Sunday was fair and hot, with the round Texas sun beating down on them. Just as Dennis had promised, the Alta Vista city pool was beautiful—a big blue jewel of water skirted by a patchwork of bright beach towels. When Jill came out of the women's dressing room, Dennis was already waiting for her. His blue swim trunks revealed a tanned, muscular body, a detail Jill filed away to share with Pam later.

Dennis grinned at her, his dark eyes catching glints of the sun. "That's a terrific, uh, *suit* you've got."

Jill laughed and flipped her hair behind her ears with her hand. "Thanks," she said. "I was thinking the same thing myself. About *your* suit, I mean."

They spread their beach towels along the warm cement and lay on their stomachs, letting the sun seep into them. When they were hot enough, they jumped into the pool. The water was so cold and wonderful, it took their breath away.

"This is terrific," Jill gasped, plunging up and down.

"You bet," Dennis said. "Want to race to the other side? Any stroke you want."

"You're on," Jill said, confident of her swimming abilities. "On the count of three?"

They counted and took off across the Olympic-size pool. Jill beat Dennis by a good three strokes. She was barely out of breath when she stopped. He was gasping. "My gosh," he said as they climbed out, "where did you learn to swim like that?"

"Runs in the family," Jill answered.

Dennis gave her a puzzled look. "What is your mother, a mermaid?"

Jill laughed. She dropped down onto her beach towel and began squirting Coppertone onto her arms. Dennis sat down beside her and she squirted his arms too. As she rubbed the lotion in, she looked out across the rippling blue water of the pool. "If I had a pool, I'd fill the whole thing with ice-cold soda—diet, of course."

Dennis laughed. "I used to have a fantasy that went something like that. Only, in my case, it was filling our entire house with popcorn."

"Buttered?" Jill asked.

"Of course," he answered. "I was a very chubby kid in those days."

Jill looked at his athletic body. "I bet," she said disbelievingly.

"No, really. I'll show you a picture sometime."

For just a minute Jill's fingers stopped rubbing suntan lotion into her arm. *Sometime*. That seemed to mean he planned to ask her out again. She smiled to herself. When she looked up, Dennis was looking at her. "Thirsty?" he asked. She nodded, and he fished in the tangle of their gear for his wallet. "Be right back," he said.

Jill watched him walk off across the crowded deck. She liked him. It wasn't the same swirling, falling-out-of-orbit feeling that she'd had for Toby, but she liked him. Besides, she thought, screwing the cap back on the suntan lotion, where had that swirling feeling led her? Nowhere. Nowhere at all.

When Dennis came back, he was carrying two Popsicles. "Cherry or banana?" he asked.

Jill's eyes lit up. "I haven't had a Popsicle for years," she said. "I love them both. Take whichever one you want."

"Want to split them?" he asked.

"Sure."

So they each took half a Popsicle, half cherry, half banana. Jill had to eat quickly to keep the sticky things from melting all over her hands. Her whole mouth turned into a refrigerator.

"Want to do something fun?" Dennis asked. He leaned closer to her. Instinctively Jill moved away a little. "No, no," he said, laughing, "trust me. This is fun, I promise." Before she could move away again, he kissed her, his cold, Popsicled mouth making contact with hers. He was right—it *was* fun.

Jill laughed. "So much for hot passion," she said.

Dennis bit off the last of his Popsicle and gave her one more funny, chilly kiss. "Hard to believe there are people who think they're too old for Popsicles, isn't it?" he said, and winked at her. "If only they knew what they're missing."

"Thanks," Jill said.

"For the Popsicle?"

"Hmmm, that too."

They laid back down on their towels, on their backs this time, face up to the sun. Through the closed lids of her eyes, Jill watched slow rainbows dancing. After a while she felt Dennis reach over and take her hand. She gave his hand a little squeeze, but she didn't change positions. She didn't want to move, didn't want to risk upsetting the perfect happiness she felt. She could lie this way forever, she thought, warm and full of sunlight, with Dennis holding her hand, gazing up at a future full of rainbows.

The End

Two days went by, and Jill couldn't decide what to do. Those two days were the worst of Jill's entire life. Kids she'd been friends with for years avoided her glance. She could walk the entire length of the first floor hallway without once hearing anybody say "Hello, Jill." For the first time since she'd moved to Westmore, she was the last to be picked for a team in gym class. It all made her terribly lonely. And it was all terribly unfair.

Even Pam seemed to be disappointed in her. Not because Pam believed Jill was anything like the Jill Farrell in Erica's scandal sheet. No; Pam was too bright for that. But Pam was a woman of action, and she was disappointed in Jill for not taking action against Erica right away. "If it were me," Pam said, "I'd find a way to get even with her—pronto."

Jill told Pam her plan about dropping Erica into a vat of chocolate syrup. "I like that," Pam said approvingly.

"Too bad it's illegal," Jill said regretfully. "I wonder what I'd get for doing it?"

Pam's dark eyebrows went up like wings. "There's not a court in the land that would convict you," she said.

Jill laughed. If it hadn't been for Pam and the loyal supporters on her campaign staff, she didn't know what she'd do. *And* Nick Donnelly, she remembered. Nick had been as good as gold, giving her rides to and from school and going out of his way to run into her between classes. Jill wondered how someone who had been such a terror in the fifth grade could have turned into someone so nice. And all without her knowing about it. Since getting over her crush on Nick back in the eighth grade, she'd scarcely noticed him. But these days she was noticing him a lot.

When he let her off in front of her house on Friday afternoon, Nick asked Jill if she had any specific plans for the weekend. "No," she told him, shaking her head. "I mean, I'm not exactly Miss Popularity around school these days." Even saying the word *popularity* made her flinch.

Nick didn't notice, or pretended not to. "Well, there's a Woody Allen double feature on channel seven—*Sleeper* and *Bananas*. We could watch it together."

"That sounds nice, Nick," Jill said. Thank God for Woody Allen, she thought. At least there was something left in the world to laugh about.

They decided to watch the movies at Jill's house. "Don't start popping the popcorn until I get there," he warned as Jill slid out of his car. "I'm an expert hand at getting all the kernels to pop."

Jill waved good-bye to him. She was glad he'd decided to come over. Even so, she couldn't help brooding about her situation at school. She laid her books down and walked into the kitchen. Her mother was sitting at the kitchen table sorting through an immense stack of coupons.

"Hi, honey," Mrs. Farrell said. She gestured toward the coupons. "Look at this—a gold mine. I swapped my dog food file with Lois Fletcher."

"Great," Jill said unenthusiastically.

Her mother looked at her a little more closely. "That's a pretty deadpan tone of voice for a Friday afternoon," she said. "Did something happen at school today?"

Jill hadn't told her family about what had happened at the assembly two days ago. Who would? she thought. It wasn't the most appealing thing in the world, telling your parents that you had suddenly become about as popular as ants at a picnic. Maybe now was the time, Jill thought. She sat down and began to recite the entire story. Thank goodness her mother knew Erica. Otherwise it would have sounded pretty unbelievable. Somewhere in the middle of the story her kid sister, Penny, came in and raided the refrigerator. Not that it was much of a raid, Jill noticed—a handful of carrot sticks and a stalk of celery. Penny sat down beside Jill and listened to the story. The sound of Penny's steady, rabbitlike crunching served as punctuation.

"I know I *should* do something about Erica," Jill said after she had finished explaining everything. "Pam thinks I should anyway. But it seems like the damage is already done. What good would come of it?"

Mrs. Farrell pushed the coupons to one side. "People have pretty short memories, honey," she said sympathetically. "Maybe you'll find that by Monday the whole thing has blown over."

"Maybe," Jill said, but she didn't hold out much hope. Maybe when you were an adult, there were so many things to think about that your mind crowded out little episodes like this, but not when you were seventeen. When you were seventeen, this was the biggest thing that could happen. By Monday nobody would have forgotten anything.

Penny finished her last carrot stick. "If I were in your class, I'd vote for you, Jill," she said.

Jill felt her eyes prickle, as if she were going to cry. She wanted to put both arms around her little sister, but she knew Penny would wrinkle her nose and squirm away. Instead, Jill said, "I'd vote for you too."

"Really? You would?" Penny's face brightened. It was like watching sunlight pour over a flat stretch of plain.

"Sure," Jill said. Watching Penny's smile was almost as good as putting her arms around her, she decided.

Nick appeared on Saturday night carrying a big Hershey bar, the kind you buy in grocery stores. They popped batches of popcorn and alternated bites of chocolate and handfuls of corn, with shrieks of laughter. Jill didn't even mind that Penny watched the first of the two movies with them.

When *Bananas* was over, Penny yawned and went to bed, leaving Jill and Nick alone in the den. Nick excused himself to use the bathroom. When he came back, he sat down close to Jill on the couch—so close that, when one of them reached for a handful of popcorn or a glass of soda, their legs brushed together. Jill hoped that that was as far as things would go. She liked Nick and was glad he'd come, but her feelings didn't go further than that. There was too much going on at school to leave time for anything else. And there was her crush on Toby. That, Jill knew, was the real reason she didn't want to get involved with Nick.

But Jill needn't have worried. Nick must have sensed her mood. He did nothing more than drape his arm over the back of the couch and brush her shoulder with the tips of his fingers from time to time. When the second movie was over, he gave her a quick kiss on the cheek and offered to pick her up for school on Monday. Jill hadn't taken the bus since the day of the assembly. She couldn't go on letting Nick chauffeur her around for the rest of her life just so she wouldn't have to face her classmates. She'd have to go back to taking the bus sometime, she decided. Monday seemed as good a day as any. When she turned down Nick's offer, he smiled and said, "See you Monday, then."

Jill tried to decide whether things at school were any better on Monday than they had been on Friday. She couldn't say for sure—kids still weren't bowling her over with hellos—but the atmosphere *seemed* a little warmer. *Maybe Mom's right after all,* Jill thought. *They can't stay mad at me forever, can they?* When Pat Harmon asked to borrow her notes in world history, Jill's spirits soared. She felt, for the first time in days, that she wasn't destined to spend the rest of her high school career as Public Enemy Number One. And if the other kids forgot about what had happened, Jill reasoned, she could too. Maybe she could get through this without confronting Erica at all.

For four whole hours—until lunchtime—Jill was in a state of something closely resembling happiness. Deciding that she might not have to face Erica was like getting an early parole from prison. She hadn't realized how much she'd been dreading it. Now a heavy weight seemed to have rolled off her back. She bounced out of her fourth-period class and headed straight for the cafeteria, eager to tell Pam about the improvement in her situation. Pam, of course, would be disappointed that there wouldn't be a showdown, but Jill was in such a cheerful mood that she felt good anyway.

Jill got to the cafeteria first and got in line, sliding her blue plastic tray along the counter and picking out chicken salad and steamed broccoli. She looked for a place to sit down and saw Toby, sitting alone at his usual spot.

If she'd been using her head, Jill decided later, she would never have done what she did. She would have marched quietly to her own table and waited for Pam, avoiding all risks. But she wasn't thinking with her head. Not when she saw Toby. Her heart took over, and she walked right up to him, her tray in her hands.

"Hi," she said, smiling.

Toby looked up. He didn't return her smile. And his eyes, which were always so bright and welcoming, were as cool as Arctic ice. "Hello, Jill," he said.

What was going on? Jill thought. At that moment she was so full of her own feelings for Toby that she didn't even think about his feelings for her. Later, when she thought about how dumb she must have looked standing there—just *standing* there—she wanted to die. Because she didn't know what to do or say, she cleared her throat and asked, "How are things going?"

"Fine," Toby said. "Just fine. I'd ask you to sit

down but I know how *popular* you are—I'm sure there are lots of people waiting for you. Don't let me keep you."

That's when it hit her. Toby had seen Erica's sheet too. And of course, with Erica's help, he believed it. Jill felt her throat tighten. "Toby, I—"

"Yes, Jill?" His voice was cold and distant and scary.

"Never mind." She turned away from him and walked as quickly as she could to the other side of the room. By the time she found an empty place at a table and sat down, tears had splashed down onto her chicken salad. That was okay, Jill told herself—she wasn't going to eat it anyway.

By the time Pam arrived, Jill had gotten through the crying stage of her crisis. Instead, the first words she said to Pam were, "I'll *kill* her."

Pam didn't have to ask who. "Good," she said. "Where'll we stash the body?"

"No," Jill continued, thinking about her plan. "Killing's too good for her. I want something slow and excruciating."

"Good heavens," Pam said, "maybe you'd better tell me what happened. It must have been a lulu."

"Lulu," Jill said, "doesn't begin to describe it." She told Pam about going up to Toby, and about the way Toby had treated her. "I mean," Jill said, "I can see why he acted that way, considering the fact that he believes *I* put out that stupid sheet. But it was terrible—I felt like he was looking straight through me."

"So you're really going to talk to Erica?" Pam asked eagerly. The idea of witnessing the slaughter made her eyes gleam. "You're not going to back down?"

"Not this time," Jill said firmly. "As soon as I can catch up with her, I'm going to let her have it."

Pam leaned back in her chair and breathed a sigh of relief. "I wish I could see the whole thing," she said. "Erica has had this coming for *years*."

Jill shook her head violently. "No witnesses," she insisted. "I don't want to make a big deal of this."

"Okay," Pam agreed. "As long as you promise to give me the blow-by-blow description when it's over."

"Don't worry," Jill assured her, "I will."

Later that day, Jill caught up with Erica between classes. "I'd like to talk to you, Erica," she said. "What would be a good time?"

Erica had a dog's sense for danger. She looked suspicious. "I'm awfully busy, Jill," she said evasively.

"This will only take a few minutes," Jill replied.

"All right, after school, then."

"Where shall we meet?"

Erica thought for a moment. "How about your campaign office?" she said.

Jill agreed. "See you then," she said, and hurried off to her next class.

She got to the campaign office two minutes after the last bell of the day rang. She wasn't going to take any chances—she didn't want Erica saying she had waited for Jill and then gone home. Jill sat in the room alone, listening to the hum of voices die away outside the door. Ten minutes passed, and Erica failed to show up. *Just like Erica,* Jill thought, *to keep me waiting.* But after another twenty minutes Jill's patience was exhausted. *That little rat,* she thought. *She's not coming at all! She's standing me up! Well, she's not going to get away with it. This time she's gone too far.*

The next morning Jill got up a half-hour early and rode into town with her father. "I have a before-school meeting," she explained to him. She didn't mention with whom. This was strictly her business, and she would take care of it her own way, Jill decided. She hadn't even told Pam what she was planning.

Fresh morning sunlight was spilling through the empty corridors of Westmore High when Jill arrived. She made her way to her own locker, gathered the books she'd need for her morning classes, and went to the second floor. She didn't know exactly which locker was Erica's, but she knew it was somewhere near the second-floor lavatories. Jill ducked into the girls' lavatory and waited, keeping the door open just a crack.

It seemed that hours passed before anything happened. Finally students began to arrive. Girls gave Jill an odd look as they pushed by her into the lavatory, but she ignored them. Her deep blue eyes scanned the length of the hallway. Finally she saw Erica. Jill waited until Erica was almost finished getting her books out of her locker, then she darted out into the hallway. "Erica," she said, grasping her rival by the elbow. "Isn't this lucky? We seem to have missed each other yesterday afternoon. Now we can have our talk."

Erica looked panic-stricken. Her face turned as pale as her white-blond hair. "I—I'll be late for English," she stammered.

But Jill didn't let go of her elbow. "Too bad," she said. Kids were buzzing past them now, and the halls were crowded. "Where shall we talk?" Jill asked. "Here?"

"No!" Erica almost shouted. "I mean—uh—it's a little noisy here, isn't it? Why don't we go to the office?"

Erica meant the room that was Toby's campaign office. It was at the end of the second-floor hallway. "Fine," Jill agreed.

They made their way through the crowded hall. Jill kept close to Erica. In case she made a break for it and tried to get away, Jill was ready to grab her.

When they got inside the campaign office, Jill closed the door behind them. She had never been in the room before. Half of it was cordoned off by a folding screen. Toby's election posters were tacked up on the screen. So was a copy of the infamous sheet. Jill crossed the room and looked at the sheet. "'Hi, I'm Jill Farrell,'" she read. She stopped and turned to Erica. "You wrote that, didn't you?"

"I don't know what you're talking about," Erica said.

"Oh, come on, Erica," Jill said. "That isn't even a good lie. You can do better than that, can't you?"

"I don't know what you're talking about," Erica repeated.

"I'm talking about the fact that you wrote this thing yourself," Jill said, "and passed it out just before the assembly last week to make me look bad. That's one of the most underhanded things I've ever heard of, Erica. I mean, you have to be really devious just to *think* of it, let alone *do* it."

Erica looked away. "You're crazy, Jill. Absolutely crazy."

"If you don't admit you did this," Jill said, her voice hard as a riverbed during drought, "I'm prepared to go to the principal and tell him what happened."

Erica's mouth dropped open. "You wouldn't!"

Jill looked at her a long moment. "Wouldn't I?" she asked. "Well, I guess you'll just have to wait and see, won't you?" She made a move toward the door. Jill wasn't sure herself whether she would make good on her threat. After all, she didn't have a shred of evidence.

But before she got to the door, she heard Erica's voice behind her, shrill with anger and fear. "What if I *did* do it?" Erica shrieked. "It's not such a big deal as all that. Cripes, you make it sound like I robbed the treasury or something."

Jill was furious, but she tried to keep her voice calm. The bell had rung, and first period was under way. If she lost control and started screaming, teachers would descend on them from all directions. "It may not be a big deal to you, Erica, but it is to me. What you did wasn't fair." That, Jill thought, was an understatement.

"*Fair?*" Erica questioned. "What would you know about *fair?* Do you think it's fair that you're so popular around here, half the kids would vote for you for dictator if you asked them to? Do you think it's fair that Toby's got such a huge crush on you that he won't even notice me? Do you think it's fair that—"

"That's enough, Erica."

The voice wasn't Jill's. The two girls looked around. Toby appeared from behind the screen. Jill felt all the blood in her body rush down to her feet. She saw Erica grab the edge of a desk with one hand.

"Toby, I—" Erica gasped.

"We'll talk about it later, Erica," he said. "I want to talk to Jill right now. *Alone*."

Jill barely heard the door open and close as Erica left the room. She looked down. When she looked up again, Toby was looking at her. "I'm sorry, Jill," he said. The sound of his voice and the look in his eyes were enough to break her heart.

"It wasn't your fault, Toby," she said.

"Yes," he said, "it was. In a way, anyway. I should have known you wouldn't have put that sheet out yourself. I should have realized Erica's devious little mind had something to do with it. I just got carried away, I guess. I mean, I wanted to win so badly, I forgot about everything else." He paused. Jill didn't say anything. She knew that if the situation were reversed, she'd feel the same way Toby did—responsible, guilty. But that didn't prepare her for what Toby said next. "I think the best thing for me to do," he said slowly, "would be to drop out of the election."

Jill jerked her head up. "*No!*" she said. "That wouldn't be fair."

"I don't think I'm in a position to ask for fairness," Toby said with a sad little smile that made Jill want to fly to him and put her arms around his neck.

Instead, she said, "I wasn't thinking of what's fair to you. I was thinking of what's fair to the voters. No matter what Erica's done, they deserve a good election. They deserve to choose."

"But I should have *known* what was going on," Toby insisted.

Jill walked across to where Toby was standing and put her hand on his shoulder. "Just make Erica admit what she's done, and I'll be happy," she said. "It's really her fault, not yours. A simple explanation to the school paper will do it." She paused. Toby still looked miserable. "After all," Jill added lightly, "you can't be expected to know every mean little thought that passes through that coyotelike mind of hers."

Toby tried to smile. "Thanks, Jill," he said. "But you know what bothers me more than Erica? Myself. How could I have believed the things she said about you?"

Jill flinched. She hoped Toby wouldn't go into detail about what those "things" were. To stop him she said, "Well, Erica can be pretty persuasive when she gets going, I guess. I mean, you're not the only one that fell for her trick. The rest of the class did too."

Now Toby did smile. "I'll see that *that* part of it's taken care of at least. If I have to tie her to the microphone, I'll make Erica admit to the whole school that she put out that sheet." He paused. "I guess people are pretty gullible, aren't they? I mean, here are these kids that have known you all your life, and all it takes is one little piece of paper and—boom!—you're on the outside looking in."

Jill nodded. That's exactly how she'd felt since last week's assembly—on the outside looking in. "That's a good way to describe it," she said.

Toby chuckled. "Oh, I've had a taste of it myself, though not in such a big way. Remember those campaign posters of mine? I got the cold shoulder from a few kids when the posters came out, and found out that somehow the rumor had got started that my dad had given me fifty dollars to spend on them."

Jill blushed. She had heard that rumor herself—and believed it. "Not true?" she asked him.

"Are you kidding?" Toby asked. "You've obviously never met my father. He believes in self-made men. If it were up to him, I'd be splitting logs and walking to school, just like Abe Lincoln. He wouldn't give me five dollars to buy votes with, much less fifty. Besides," he added, and winked at Jill, "do I look like the kind of man who would stoop to wowing the voters with my wealth?"

Jill laughed. It felt wonderful. "Then where *did* those posters come from?" she asked. "They *were* pretty impressive."

"Weren't they though?" Toby replied. "They were another scheme of Erica's. She made some kind of deal with the printer. I don't know exactly what. I guess it's another point I overlooked."

All of a sudden Jill realized how close she was standing to him. Close enough to catch the spicy scent of his after-shave. Close enough to see that he had a very light mole on the right side of his chin. It was funny. She'd wanted to stand this close to Toby for a long time. And now that she was, she didn't know what to say. She took a step backward. "Imagine," she said, looking for a new topic of conversation. "Imagine Erica thinking that I was standing between the two of you, keeping her from starting a romance."

Toby's voice was soft and gentle. "Erica isn't wrong about everything, Jill."

Jill looked up at him, her blue eyes showing her surprise. She opened her mouth and started to ask a question, then closed it again.

Toby seemed to know what she'd been about to ask

and nodded his head in reply. "That's one thing Erica is absolutely right about, Jill," he said. "I *do* like you, and Erica knows it. In fact, I'd planned to ask you out as soon as the campaign was over."

It took Jill a few minutes to recover. "Well," she said, "I hope you haven't changed your plans about *that*." Toby took a step toward her. They were standing close together again. And this time Jill knew what to say. "I'd like to go out with you, Toby," she said. And just in case he didn't believe her, she smiled at him.

"Even after all this?" he asked.

Jill nodded.

If someone had asked her to predict when, if ever, she and Toby would kiss for the first time, she would never in a million years have picked eight-forty-five on a Tuesday morning. But that was how it happened. Toby's arms went around her and held her tight. "You've got my vote, Jill," he said, and kissed her.

She kissed him back, her hand rising to touch his curly, golden-blond hair. The election was still a week away but, no matter what happened, it could never top this. *Toby and Jill,* she thought, snuggling against his chest. Toby and Jill—she already had a place on the winning ticket.

The End

Jill was determined not to make an issue out of what had happened. She couldn't bear dragging the whole thing out in front of everyone and couldn't bear the thought of humiliating Toby that way.

"Stubborn pride," Pam said with an exasperated sigh, her eyes fixed on Jill like black beads. "That's all it is, just stubborn pride. How are kids going to know you didn't print that thing unless you tell them so? Or make Erica tell them? You're sealing the coffin on your chances of becoming president. You know that, don't you?"

"If people don't know me well enough by now to know I wouldn't print anything like that," Jill replied firmly, "then I don't want their votes."

"You're nuts," Pam said.

"Maybe," Jill replied. But she didn't change her mind. She had made her decision, and she was going to stick with it, no matter what happened.

But "no matter what" turned out to be a lot tougher than Jill had imagined. Erica's stunt had done more than make her classmates decide not to vote for her; it had made them decide not to speak to her as well. She'd never—ever—in her whole life felt so rejected. "It's like having bubonic plague," she complained to Nick Donnelly.

"Don't worry," Nick replied with a grin. "I'm immune."

Jill smiled at him. Except for Pam and Tim and the kids on her campaign staff, Nick was the only person who hadn't turned against her. In fact, Nick had gone out of his way to show her that he was on her side. "I guess I can count on your vote then, can't I?" Jill asked.

Nick nodded and finished the last forkful of his hamburger casserole. "You sure can," he said.

"Good," Jill said grimly. "I think that brings me up to a total of twenty-eight votes. Twenty-nine, counting my own." She looked at the barely touched food on her plate. She couldn't help it—she felt as if everyone in the cafeteria were staring at her. Not that Westmore High's hamburger casserole was a high point even when you *had* an appetite, she decided. "Can we go now, Nick?" she asked. "Please? I—uh—I have to check on a book in the library."

It was a pretty obvious fib, but Nick pretended not to notice. "Sure," he said, getting to his feet. "Let's split."

Jill waited for two days for things to get better at school. Then the weekend arrived, and she worked on hoping that things would improve by Monday. Weekends were always good for clearing people's minds, she knew. Particularly if they were rowdy. But that weekend in Westmore was particularly peaceful, and Monday at school turned out to be no different for Jill than Thursday and Friday had been.

"This is ridiculous," Pam fumed as they walked through the lunch line together without a single word being spoken to them. "Absolutely ridiculous— and it's all Erica's fault."

Jill tried to calm Pam down. "It can't last forever," she said.

"No," Pam said, "you're right, it can't. We'll be graduating a year from now. That should put an end to it." She paused. "I *wish* you'd talk to Erica about this."

"Pam, let's not go over all that again. I've told you a hundred times—I'm not going to talk to her."

Resigned, Pam ate her lunch in silence while Jill picked at hers.

Between sixth and seventh period Jill ran to her campaign office with a position paper she'd written in afternoon study hall. She couldn't retract Erica's publication, but she could try to lessen the damage by putting out an authentic statement of her own. She left the paper with one of her campaign workers and hurried back out into the hallway. She was on the first floor, just in front of the administrative offices, when she ran into Pam. "Hi," Jill started to say, but stopped in the middle of the word. She couldn't believe it. Erica was with Pam, walking right beside her.

Pam looked embarrassed. "Hi, Jill," she said, and hurried past her.

Jill walked to her last class in a state of confusion. What was Pam doing with Erica? She knew Pam far too well to doubt her loyalty. Still, there must be an awfully interesting story behind it all, Jill reasoned. She could hardly wait to find out what it was. And, as it happened, she didn't have to wait long at all. As soon as the afternoon announcements came on the public address system, the vice-principal said there was a special message for the junior class. The next thing Jill knew, Erica's voice came on.

"This is Erica Babcock," she said. There was a pause—a long one—before she continued. "Well, most of you probably know that I'm working on Toby

Martin's campaign for him. And believe me, this is going to come as much of a surprise to him as it will to the rest of you. I just hope you remember that. I mean, Toby had nothing to do with any of this." Jill stared at her open notebook. Oh, gosh, she thought, Erica's going to tell everyone what she did. Poor Toby. Jill glanced around the room at her classmates. They were listening intently. Erica cleared her throat and continued. "Last week I did something pretty dumb. It was a joke, really—or supposed to be—but it backfired. At the assembly last Wednesday a certain piece of paper—concerning one of the candidates for senior class president—got handed out. I . . . uh . . . I was the one who wrote that paper." The room—the whole school, it seemed—was so quiet, you could have heard a pin drop. "Like I said, it was meant to be a joke. I never thought anyone would believe it. I thought it over and decided I had to tell the truth, explain what really happened. I'm really sorry."

I'll bet she's sorry, Jill thought. *I'll bet it was meant to be a joke. That little guttersnipe.* But Jill was used to feeling angry at Erica. She wasn't used to feeling angry at Pam. Jill knew from the moment she heard Erica's voice on the P.A. system that Pam was behind the confession. Pam had gone to Erica and somehow pressured her into admitting what she'd done. Jill felt betrayed and angry. How could Pam have done that to her? Jill had told her at least a dozen times how she felt and why, and Pam had deliberately taken matters into her own hands.

"How could you?" Jill asked her. She had flown to Pam's locker as soon as the final bell rang and waited there for her. "You knew I wanted to let the whole thing drop—that I didn't want to get involved in Erica's dirty tricks."

"You didn't get involved," Pam said. "And neither did Toby. This was strictly between me and Erica, campaign manager to campaign manager."

"But you *knew* how I felt," Jill repeated. Her voice was shaking. She blinked back tears.

Pam threw her books into the locker with a crash and whirled to face Jill. "What are you angry at *me* for?" she demanded, her dark eyes flashing. "You should be thanking me. Do you think it was easy, getting Erica to admit what she'd done? Thanks to me you've got a shot at being class president again."

Pam slammed her locker door and walked away before Jill could stop her. Jill leaned against the row of lockers. She felt two tears roll slowly down her cheeks. She and Pam had been friends for years, and they'd never had an argument before. Not an argument like this one anyway. Jill wondered if they'd ever be friends again. She looked down at her T-shirt and saw the two spots the tears had made. She hadn't cried in school since she was six years old. Someone passed her and said, "Hi, Jill." She didn't look up. Now that Erica had made her confession, she realized, she was no longer Public Enemy Number One. That was a victory of sorts, she thought. But somehow it didn't feel like one.

Jill felt a gentle hand on her shoulder. She looked up, wiping her wet cheeks with the tips of her fingers. It was Nick. "Miss Farrell?" he said, making a mock bow. "Donnelly's limo service is here. Like a ride home?"

Jill nodded. Nick had been so nice to her these past few days, it was impossible not to like him. Most of all she liked his gentleness and his way of not pushing her. She liked the fact that he didn't once ask her what had happened, or why—all the way home—she kept reaching up to wipe tears from her eyes.

That night, as soon as she was finished eating dinner, Jill went to her room and buried herself in her homework. Thank goodness for *Macbeth*, she thought. It was so difficult to read, it was impossible to think about anything else. And thinking about anything else was exactly what Jill wanted to avoid.

She plowed her way through the first act and had just begun the second when she heard her kid sister Penny's heavy cowboy boots clomping up the stairs. The boots came down the hallway and stopped in front of the door to Jill's room. The door swung open and Jill looked up from her Shakespeare. "Thanks for knocking," she said.

"Mom sent me up here," Penny said. "To get you. There's some dumb boy downstairs. He says he wants to see you."

Jill stood up. The Shakespeare book slid to the floor with a thump. "Well, who is it?" she asked.

"I don't know," Penny answered, folding her arms across her flat chest. "Just some dumb boy."

Jill checked her reflection in the mirror. Good— there were no stray traces of ballpoint pen in sight, no smudges of wayward mascara. She smoothed her hair with one hand and started down the stairs. *Some dumb boy.* Why couldn't Penny be more precise? she wondered. Oh, well, Jill mused. It was probably Nick or one of the guys who was working on her campaign. A sudden flutter of fear ran through her.

Maybe it was Pam's boyfriend, Tim, wanting to know why she had been so mean to Pam.

But it wasn't Nick *or* Tim, Jill saw. She came to the bottom of the stairs and froze. "Hello," she said at last. She didn't know what else she was expected to say.

Toby took a step toward her. His hair was damp, as if he'd just taken a shower. It fell over his forehead in little golden spirals. "I'm sorry I didn't call before I came over," he said. "I was afraid you'd hang up on me."

Jill shook her head. She couldn't imagine hanging up on Toby. Ever. "Do you—uh—would you like to come in?" she asked.

He looked relieved. He even smiled at her. "That'd be nice, Jill. I mean, I think we need to talk."

Jill led him into the den. Thank heavens *Dynasty* wasn't on, she thought, or *Dallas*. Penny would have been glued to the TV set, and even the threat of imminent death wouldn't have moved her. As it was, the set was off, and Penny was nowhere in sight. "We can talk in here," Jill said. She sat down on the imitation leather couch, which had a longhorn design embroidered on the backrest. She sat with her back just touching the tip of the left horn. Toby sat all the way on the other end of the couch, on the right tip of the horn. For a few minutes neither of them said anything. Jill poked her index finger in and out of a tiny hole in the knee of her blue jeans.

It was Toby who broke the silence. "I think I should tell you," he said, not looking directly at her, "that Erica isn't my campaign manager anymore. I asked her to resign."

Jill pulled her finger out of the hole in her jeans

and smoothed the loose threads. "You did?" she asked, looking at him. "Really?"

Toby nodded. "It was the least I could do," he said. There was another long silence. When Toby spoke again, his voice sounded dry. "I didn't know that Erica was the one who handed that sheet out. Honest."

"I never thought you did," Jill told him.

For the first time Toby looked directly into her eyes. "You didn't?" he asked.

"Of course not," Jill said. "I know Erica, and I know the way she feels about me."

Toby looked puzzled. "You do? Who told you?"

"Who told me?" Jill echoed. "Nobody told me," she said. "Nobody needed to. Erica's hated me for years."

"Oh, that," Toby said, leaning back against the couch. "I thought you meant—"

Jill looked at him. "Meant what?"

A slow flush started at the collar of Toby's blue shirt and rose to his cheeks. If Jill hadn't seen it with her own eyes, she would never have believed it: Toby Martin, blushing. She kept her eyes on him, and when he didn't say anything, she asked her question again. "Meant what, Toby?"

"Well—uh—gosh, this is the worst way in the world to . . . oh, well, here goes." He turned sideways on the couch so that his whole body faced her. "Look, Jill," he said, "I like you a lot. That day I asked you to be my campaign manager, I was really planning to ask you out. I don't know, for some reason I panicked. I mean, you're the only girl in school who's ever really intimidated me, I guess. And I thought, what if she won't go out with me? So instead, I asked you to manage my campaign. I thought I could sort of ease into it that way. Then you decided to run against me, and I couldn't very well ask you out then, could I? So I decided to ask you out as soon as the campaign was over. Well, somehow Erica found out how I feel about you. Don't ask me how—I think the girl's part bloodhound. She didn't take it very well. I mean, I guess she likes me or something. So I knew she had it in for you—it just never occurred to me that she'd do something like this because of it." Toby stopped. He tilted his head back and looked up at the ceiling. "I feel like a complete idiot," he said.

Jill studied his fine profile. "*I* feel marvelous," she said.

Toby's head snapped down. He looked at her. "You do?" he asked.

"Yeah," she said, nodding. "I do. Absolutely marvelous."

Toby's eyebrows crinkled together in a puzzled frown. "Why?" he asked.

"Could we back up to what you were saying a few minutes ago? That part about you liking me and wanting to ask me out? Could we back up to your deciding to ask me out the Friday after the school elections?"

Toby looked at her. "Sure," he said. "We could back up to that."

"Good," Jill said. "I accept."

A slow grin spread across Toby's face. "Hey, that's great," he said. "*Great!*"

Somehow—Jill never knew exactly how—they ended up together in the center of the couch, right in the middle of the longhorns. Toby's arm was around her, and she snuggled against him. "I've wanted you to ask me out forever," she said.

"For*ever*?" he asked, lifting his eyebrows. "Must have been a pretty long wait."

"I'm patient," Jill said.

Toby put his thumb under her chin and raised her head. "I'm not," he said, and kissed her. "Which is why I'd better get going. After all, the elections aren't until next week. I've got more than a week to wait for our date!"

"You can do it," Jill teased.

"I'll *have* to," he replied. His confidence was back, and once again he was the same old Toby—the Toby no one could get to. But just for a moment Jill knew, *she* had gotten to him. She would never forget the look she had seen in his eyes—sad and hopeful at the same time. For the rest of her life, she thought, whenever she remembered that look, she would remember Toby and the special way he made her feel.

She walked him to the front door and out onto the porch. It was warm and still out, and the hot dry air of summer was already settling over the Texas flatlands. Insects buzzed around the yellow globe of the porch light. Toby put his arms around her and she leaned against him. "Good night," she murmured.

"Night," he replied. Neither of them tried to pull away though. Toby looked down into her eyes, and Jill knew he was going to kiss her again. After the kiss, she hugged him hard and he hugged her back.

"This must be what they mean when they refer to 'the loyal opposition,'" Jill said. Toby laughed, kissed her once more—a light kiss on the forehead this time—and bounded down the steps. Jill watched him back his car out of the driveway. Everything was perfect, she thought as she stepped back into the house. Perfect.

Then she stopped. No, everything wasn't perfect. There was one big thing in her life that wasn't perfect at all. She headed back up the stairs to her room, picked up the receiver of her white push-button phone and pressed the seven digits of Pam's number.

The phone in the Nagle house rang three times before anyone answered it. "Hello, Jill," Mrs. Nagle said when she heard Jill's voice. "Just a second—I'll tell Pam you're calling."

"Please don't," Jill said quickly. "I mean, just tell her there's a phone call, okay? It's—it's sort of a surprise." Jill didn't want to risk Pam hanging up on her, or not coming to the phone at all. Jill knew that her best friend—or *former* best friend—had a temper like a firecracker. She might still be smoldering from this afternoon.

But Pam's voice was calm when she picked up the receiver and heard Jill's voice. "Hello, Jill," she said coolly. "I thought you might call."

"You did?" Jill asked.

"Of course. I know what happened, and I know why you're calling."

There was no way, Jill thought. Even Pam, who usually knew everything, couldn't have known what had just happened with Toby. This is going to be interesting, Jill decided. "So why don't you tell me?" she said into the telephone receiver.

"Tell you what?" Pam questioned.

"Tell me what I was going to tell you."

It sounded kind of funny, but Pam refused to laugh. Her temper had cooled, all right—right down to the freezing level. "Okay," she said. "For starters you were going to tell me that Toby went to Erica this afternoon and asked her to resign as campaign manager."

Amazing, Jill thought. Absolutely amazing. The girl was clairvoyant. "How did you know that?"

"Never mind. I have my sources," Pam said proudly.

"Apparently. What next?"

"Isn't it obvious?" Pam asked. "Erica went behind Toby's back, he asked her to resign. According to you, I did the same thing. Aren't you going to ask me to resign?"

Wrong! Jill thought. The great clairvoyant's career was over. "That's about the last thing I was going to ask you," Jill said.

For the first time Pam's voice softened a little. "Really? Well, what do you want, then?"

"First of all I want to apologize," Jill said. "Even though I still don't agree with what you did—going to Erica without telling me first—I know you were only doing it for my own good."

"At least you admit that possibility," Pam said. "But just for the record I'm sorry too. I mean, I'd hate for us to stop being friends. All the way home tonight, I kept thinking that, if you never spoke to me again, I'd probably have to spend the rest of my high school days eating lunch with Mary Ellen Waters or somebody like that."

"A fate worse than death," Jill said. She even dared to try a little laugh, and Pam joined her. Jill continued. "That's not the only reason I called though."

"Oh?"

"Nope. I also wanted to tell you what happened *after* Erica resigned, and give you a chance to say 'I told you so.'"

"Oh, this is going to be good, isn't it?" Pam said, her voice ripe with enthusiasm. "Hang on a sec, I want to switch to the upstairs phone so I can have a little privacy."

Jill told Pam everything that had happened with Toby. Telling about it—describing the way he looked and the way she felt when he leaned over and kissed her—was almost like having it happen all over again. It was so delicious, Jill stretched the story out as long as she possibly could. When she glanced at the clock on her night table, she was shocked to see that it was almost midnight.

"Yipes," she said. "I'd better get off or I'll never get up tomorrow."

"Yeah, me too," Pam agreed. "I mean, my brother's been pacing back and forth for the last half hour. He wants to call his girlfriend before she goes to sleep." She paused. "I'm glad you called, Jill. I was so afraid we'd just walk around school all day tomorrow sort of busily avoiding each other. Hey, you know what? In exactly fifteen minutes it'll be Tuesday. And a week from Tuesday—"

"I know, I know," Jill interrupted. "A week from Tuesday is the election. I wonder who'll win."

It was a good thing it *was* so late, Jill thought. Otherwise she would have lain awake for hours, thinking about Toby and her—and wondering which of them was going to win the school election.

♡

If you think Toby wins the election, go to page 130.

If you think Jill wins, go to page 144.

Jill walked from the main conference hall back to the little one-room cabin she shared with Mrs. Ingersoll. Dust rose around her shoes and hot, pure sunlight warmed her hair. Red River was a beautiful place, she thought to herself. It had been a summer camp once, and it still had the unmistakable air of a camp about it. Jill wondered if that was why adults seemed to love it so much—because it reminded them of going away to camp as children.

There were other reasons to love Red River, of course. The man-made lake that sparkled like a blue mirage at the foot of the campgrounds, the chance to be with other people who liked to write, the inspiring lecture she had just heard on plot construction and the short story.

Jill's head was full of ideas from the lecture. Always before, she had just set out with a beginning and a vague ending in mind when she wrote a story. Now she saw that she wanted to do much more than that—she wanted to lay out each piece of the story and tie it firmly to another piece of the story before she started writing. It was like making a quilt, she thought—arranging different things so they joined together to make a finished pattern.

But her eagerness to start a new story was only part of the reason she was hurrying toward her cabin. The other reason was lodged in her heart, not her head. She had been at the writers' conference for three days, and she hoped there would be a letter from Dennis waiting for her. She swung the screen door open and went inside. Mrs. Ingersoll, her dark hair styled incongruously in two pigtails, was gathering a stack of papers and three glossy-covered paperback books.

"Hi, Jill," the teacher said, smiling. "I'm off to give my 'Writing for Young Adults' lecture again. Are you down for that one today?"

Jill shook her head. "Tomorrow." She paused and glanced at the desk they shared. "Any mail for me?"

Mrs. Ingersoll was almost out the door. "Oh," she said, "I put it on your bed. See you later."

Jill didn't even hear the door close behind her. She raced to the bed and looked at the two envelopes, one blue and one white. The blue one, with flowers decorating the envelope flap, was from her mother. She laid it aside and examined the white one. Her heart fell. It was from Pam.

Why hadn't Dennis written? she wondered, flopping down on her bed and slowly opening her letters. He'd promised he would—absolutely *promised*.

Her mind flew back to the night that promise was made. It was four days ago, the night before she had left town. Dennis had been in a quiet mood all night. *Sulky*, in fact, was the word that had come to mind. Even though he had told her over and over again that he wasn't mad at her for going to the conference and missing the final play-off games, she knew that he wasn't glad about it either. He was disappointed. And whether he meant to or not, he was taking his disappointment out on her by spoiling their last night together. When he moved to kiss her good night, she refused and kept refusing until he promised to write her.

At best, Jill thought, it was a promise made under

duress. A promise he apparently had no intention of keeping. Well, she wasn't going to let it ruin her whole week at Red River. She couldn't spend her whole life doing things that other people—boys in particular—wanted her to do. She had learned that lesson with Toby. She was no Mary Gardner, and never would be. Even so, there was a little dark spot of worry on her heart. What if things between her and Dennis were never the same again? What if, in the brief week she was gone, he decided it was time to go out with somebody new?

Jill closed her eyes. If he broke up with her just because she did something that was important to her, she told herself, she didn't want him anyway. She tried very hard to convince herself that that was true.

She read both letters and then opened her notebook. She would write. She'd read once that great art came from great disappointment in life. She wondered if that covered great disappointment in love too.

It was too hot in the little cabin to work. Besides, she couldn't get comfortable. Sitting at the desk reminded her of school, and lying on her stomach on the bed made her want to take a nap. So she left the cabin in search of some quiet place outdoors. She found it at the foot of a large tree that looked out across the lake. Sitting down, she opened her notebook and began to write.

Jill spent the next hour alternately working to fill two pages and watching a caterpillar struggle to make its way over the toe of her tennis shoe. She felt a lot of sympathy for the caterpillar. She was considering giving it a helping hand when she heard a crunch in the grass behind her.

"Is this a private tree, or can anyone join?" a voice said.

Jill looked up. She saw a young man who, she knew, was part of the conference too. She thought his name was Larry Peters and through careful study had decided that, except for herself, he was probably the youngest person at the conference. "Have a seat," she said, "just don't squash my caterpillar." She pointed to the toe of her shoe.

Larry sat down beside her. He wasn't handsome, she thought, but he had a nice face and clear brown eyes. "Your name's Jill, isn't it?" he asked, breaking off a stem of wild grass.

Jill nodded. "You're psychic," she teased.

"No," he said, "just curious. I asked about you." His face was especially nice when he smiled, Jill thought, which he was doing now.

She smiled back. "What did you want to know about? My criminal record? I hope they kept *that* a secret."

"You just seemed so young to be here," he answered. "So I asked."

Jill nodded. "They had to waive the age requirements for me."

"So I heard," Larry said. "I suppose that means you're a super writer."

Jill didn't say anything. Thinking of the messy, imperfect two pages she'd just been struggling with, she didn't feel super at all. Larry changed the subject. "I'm glad you're here," he said. "I was afraid I was going to be the youngest one, and there wouldn't be anybody to talk to. That's why I've been hoping we'd land in some of the same lectures together."

They compared notes and discovered they'd both signed up for Mrs. Ingersoll's seminar the next day. "That's great," Larry said. "Now I know for sure I'll see you again."

Jill looked around the campgrounds. There were forty cabins, a main conference hall, a main dining hall, and a canteen that was open three hours a day. There were two vehicles on the property and one dusty ten-mile road that lead to the nearest town. All in all, it was an extremely small world. "I think that's a pretty safe bet," she said. "After all, how far could I go?"

They both laughed. Their laughter was interrupted by the clanging of an old school bell, the signal for lunch. Larry smiled, got to his feet, and offered her a hand up. "As long as you're stuck here," he said, grinning, "want to join me for lunch?"

"Sure," Jill answered. "Just let me dump this notebook in my cabin."

Over lunch Jill learned that Larry was just one year older than she was. He had graduated from a high school in Amarillo, on the other side of the state, and in the fall he'd begin his freshman year at Southern Methodist University in Dallas. He wanted to be a writer, he explained, but he wasn't going to major in English—he was going to study history because he thought a writer should know about more than "just books."

"That's an interesting approach," Jill said, and meant it. She liked Larry. She liked him because he was nice and because, without knowing it, he had come along at just the right moment. Talking to him made it easier not to brood about Dennis.

Neither Jill nor Larry talked much about their life

at home or their friends, but Jill supposed he had a girlfriend. She wondered if the girlfriend was going to SMU too. She didn't ask questions though. Why go looking for answers that would only complicate things?

There was an optional lecture that night—"Writing Comedy for Television"—and Jill and Larry decided to go together. After the lecture Jill excused herself for a minute and went to use one of the three public pay phones on the grounds. Her pocket weighted down with quarters, she dialed Dennis's home number. After two rings his mother answered the phone. "I'm sorry, Jill," Mrs. Rhodes said, "Dennis isn't home."

Jill felt a stab of disappointment. "Oh," she said. "Well, how's the team doing?"

"They won in the semifinals yesterday," Mrs. Rhodes told her. "They'll be in the final game tomorrow."

"That's terrific," Jill said. Her voice sounded flat and unenthusiastic. "Terrific," she repeated.

"Well," Mrs. Rhodes said, "we were all sure they'd make it."

The operator's voice clicked into the line and told Jill to deposit more money.

"Look," Jill said, "I've got to go now. Will you tell Dennis I called? Will you wish him luck for me?"

"Of course, Jill. I'm sure he'll appreciate it."

Jill hung up the telephone. She wondered if Mrs. Rhodes was right—she wondered if Dennis would appreciate hearing from her. She hoped so.

Jill spent much of the rest of the week with Larry. They were friends. Not hand-holding, kissing, head-over-heels friends, but friends. And, just now, that was what she needed more than anything. Because the rest of the week passed without a single card or phone call from Dennis. Jill thought that he would at least get in touch with her after the big game and share the results with her, but he didn't. It made her feel left out, rejected, as if he simply didn't need her anymore.

As she packed her suitcase to go home she wondered what she'd find when she got back. Well, she told herself grimly, if she was doomed to spend the whole summer alone, she'd make the best use of her time and write a novel. She'd learned a lot about writing in the short week she'd been away.

Just as she was getting into Mrs. Ingersoll's car, Larry came running up. "Gosh," he said, "I can't believe you almost got away. I want to give you my address. Maybe we can write to each other. I've also," he added, "got a present for you." He handed her a paperback copy of *Anna Karenina,* the book he'd been reading all week. "It's a little dog-eared," he apologized.

"But it's your book," Jill said.

"That's okay," he said. "I'll get another copy. I want you to have this one."

"Thanks, Larry," Jill said. Impulsively she lifted her chin and kissed him on the cheek. "I'll write, I promise."

"Not just letters," he called after her. "Write stories, too, promise!"

"I will," she called out the car window.

She rode all the way back to Westmore with the copy of *Anna Karenina* on her lap. Once, when they stopped for gas and Mrs. Ingersoll went to use the rest room, she opened the cover and began to read.

Happy families are all alike, it said; *every unhappy family is unhappy in its own way.* Jill closed the book and thought. Happy people are all alike; every unhappy person is unhappy in his—or *her*—own way. Maybe Tolstoi knew something at that.

Her mother had planned a special dinner for Jill's first night back: barbecued spare ribs, cucumber salad, and chocolate cake for dessert. Her family wanted to know all about the conference—what she'd done there, what kind of people she'd met, whether or not she'd learned enough to become a great writer. "Sure," she told them. "I'm going to start producing terrific novels first thing tomorrow morning. You can be my agent, Dad."

Her father rubbed his hands together and winked at her. "Great," he said. "What's my starting salary?"

"Well—uh—so far . . . what's fifteen percent of nothing?"

"Nothing," her father said, laughing. "Of course, that doesn't take accrued interest into account."

Jill laughed with him. She had missed her family. She hadn't even realized it until just now, but she had. She'd even missed the sound of Penny's cowboy boots ringing through the house like cannon fire.

They were halfway through dessert when the telephone rang. "I'll get it," Jill said, jumping up from the picnic table. She raced across the patio and up the steps. She grabbed the kitchen extension on the third ring.

"Hello?" she gasped. She was completely out of breath.

"Gosh," a familiar voice said. "I knew you'd be

glad to hear from me, but I didn't think you'd be breathless with anticipation."

"Dennis? Is that you?"

"Hmmm," he said. "Who exactly were you expecting? How many other boys do you know?"

"But you didn't write to me," she said. The words slipped out of her mouth before she could stop them. There was no point in trying to hide her disappointment or her sudden anger. "You promised you would," she said, "and you didn't. Not once."

His voice turned serious. "I know, Jill. I'm sorry. Will you give me a chance to explain? I could be in Westmore in thirty minutes."

"Okay," she agreed.

"Just admit one thing, will you?" Dennis asked.

"What?"

"Even though I *was* a rat and didn't write, you did miss me, didn't you—just a little?"

"Yes," she said. "I missed you. A lot."

Jill hung up the phone. By the time Dennis pulled up in their driveway a half hour later, she had already forgotten she was angry at him for not writing. She only remembered that she had missed him and was glad to see him.

They sat on the old-fashioned swing on the front porch of the house, staring off into the dark velvet night. Dennis's arm was around her shoulder, and Jill rested her head lightly against him.

"I really *am* sorry I didn't write, Jill," he said for the twentieth time. "It was childish, I know. I was just so disappointed that you weren't going to see me in the play-off games. I thought to myself, if she isn't going to keep her promise to see me play, why should I keep my promise to write her? By the time I got it through my thick skull that I *wanted* to write to you, the week was almost over and it was too late."

Jill put her hand up to his face, feeling his skin and the hint of razor stubble. "I like your thick head," she said. "It's good protection against beanballs." He laughed and tightened his arm around her shoulders. They sat in silence for a few more minutes, swaying gently forward and backward in the old swing. "So tell me," Jill said at last, "did you win or lose the game?"

The swing went back and forth three times before he answered. "We lost," he said. "And I made a terrific fielding error."

"I'm sorry," Jill said.

"Yeah," Dennis answered. "Me too."

"Well," Jill said, "it's like my dad always says about the Astros—wait till next year."

Dennis chuckled softly. "It's only a game anyway. It's not nearly as important as this."

"What?" Jill asked.

"This. You know, sitting here. Being together."

"Oh, that," Jill said.

"Yeah, that," Dennis answered. "And this too." He raised her chin and kissed her. He kissed her mouth and her temples and the bottoms of her ears.

"Mmmm," she said, "I really love the 'this' part of all this."

They both laughed. After a while Dennis asked, "Are you happy?"

"Mm-hmm," Jill answered.

"Me too."

"Then we've got a lot in common, haven't we?"

"I hope so."

Cradled in the gently rocking swing, they kissed again. It was true, she thought. Happy people were all alike.

The End

Jill spread the striped beach blanket on the hot fine-textured sand, slipped off her cut-offs and her sandals, and flopped down on her stomach.

"Hungry yet?" Dennis asked.

Jill shook her head. It was not quite noon, and the beach at Five Mile Lake, which would be packed two hours from now, was still relatively empty. Jill could see Pam and Tim wading into the lake, laughing and splashing handfuls of water at each other. They'd left her house at ten thirty that morning and made the entire trip on bicycles. Her thighs ached from the effort, but she wasn't hungry.

"I'm starved," Dennis said. "Ravenous."

"Have something, then," she said lazily, letting the sun soak into her body.

Dennis sighed and shook his head. "I'll wait," he said. He flopped down beside her on the blanket. When she opened her eyes, his warm brown eyes were staring straight at her.

"Hi," she said, and smiled.

Dennis reached out and touched her cheek. "I'm going to miss you when you go to that writers' thing."

She turned so he couldn't see her, facedown against the blanket, her nose rubbing the thick, nubby cotton. She was smiling. Then she turned her back to face him again. "I decided not to go," she said. "Didn't I tell you?"

Dennis jerked his head up in surprise. "No, you didn't tell me. That's great." He thought about it for a moment. "It's great for me, anyway. Why did you decide not to go? Did your parents think it cost too much?"

Jill shook her head. "No. I decided not to go, that's all."

Slowly Dennis turned on his side. His dark eyebrows drew together. "I hope you're not missing the conference just because *I* want you to be here for the play-offs. I mean, I *do* want you here, but what I really want is for you to do what *you* want to do." He paused. "Did that make any sense?"

She smiled. "It made perfect sense," she said. "And you don't have to worry—I *am* doing what I want to do. I want to see you win the title."

He still looked worried. "Are you sure?" he asked. "I mean, have you thought about this for a while? You can still change your mind, you know."

Jill turned to face him, shifting her balance to her hip and propping her chin on her hand. "I have thought about it," she said, "and I'm not going to change my mind. I'll go to the writers' conference next year if I still want to. Besides, missing that conference doesn't mean I can't work on my writing, does it? I can set aside time this summer—so many hours a week, depending on what kind of job I get, to work on it."

Dennis cupped her sleek warm hair in his hand. "I'm glad," he said. His hand slid down her head to the nape of her neck. "Really glad," he said, and kissed her.

Jill thought of that old movie that came on television every year, *Love Story,* and the line in it—"Love means never having to say you're sorry." She didn't know if that was true or not. She doubted that it was. But one thing she did know: Sometimes love meant having to learn to compromise.

The Alta Vista team beat Tella in the semifinals and went on to face the Greenwood Warriors for the final play-off game. Jill got up early on the morning of the fifteenth and dressed carefully. She was superstitious about clothes and felt that whatever she wore would influence the outcome of the game. Finally she settled on the outfit she'd been wearing the day she met Dennis for the first time: khaki shorts and a plaid shirt. For extra luck, she wore her silver necklace with the rocking horse charm on it.

"Keep your fingers crossed," she told her parents as she left the house.

"We will, honey," her father assured her.

"What time do you think you'll get home?" Mrs. Farrell asked. "Will you be here for dinner?"

Jill shook her head. "I *hope* not," she said. "If Alta Vista wins, there's going to be a big party. If they lose, I don't know what Dennis will want to do."

"Well," Mr. Farrell said, "tell Dennis good luck from us."

"I will," Jill assured him.

It was a bright, clear day outside. Perfect for baseball, Jill thought as she backed the Omni out of the garage. Perfect for victory. She hated to admit it, but she was almost as nervous about the game as Dennis was. She'd done a bit of scouting on her own by asking Pam's boyfriend, Tim, what he thought of the Greenwood team. They were good opponents, Tim thought. They would certainly give Alta Vista a run for its money—especially a heavy-hitting fielder named Reinhart. Jill didn't pass this bit of information along to Dennis. He kept telling her that he was certain—*certain*—they could beat Greenwood. But, no matter how firmly he said it, Jill always saw a cloud of worry in his eyes.

The bleachers were nearly full by the time Jill arrived at the game. Mr. and Mrs. Rhodes spotted her and began waving and calling her name. She climbed up to them. "Thanks for saving a place for me," she said, sitting down beside Dennis's mother. "Is Dennis nervous?"

"Does the sun rise in the east?" Mr. Rhodes asked. He looked like a slightly older version of Dennis, with gray fringing the edges of his dark hair.

"He told us at breakfast that he wasn't nervous at all," Mrs. Rhodes said. "Then he poured syrup all over his scrambled eggs."

Jill laughed. "I guess we're *all* nervous," she said. She liked the Rhodeses. They weren't like some kids' parents, who always made you feel that you were somehow a source of unmeasured danger and potential corruption. They were nice, like Dennis himself, and it was easy to be with them. If she had to sit through this entire game alone, Jill thought, she'd go nuts. She was glad the Rhodeses had come.

The game got off to a slow start, going the first three innings without a runner getting past first base. Then, in Alta Vista's fourth inning, the leadoff batter doubled to center field. The pitcher walked the next man, and the next batter advanced the runners on a sacrifice fly. The crowd came to life. With runners on second and third and only one away, it seemed certain that the home team would be first on the scoreboard. But the next batter struck out. Jill knew enough about baseball to know that, in this situation, a strikeout was one of the worst things that could happen. It was a wasted out, not even advancing the runners. Besides that, it gave the opposing pitcher confidence. Now there was only one out left. Alta Vista needed a solid base hit to score even one run.

Dennis was the next batter up. Jill watched him knocking the dirt off his cleats with the end of his bat. She made a mental note to remember to ask him, later, whether he did that for a real reason or just to relieve the tension of coming to the plate.

The first pitch was a ball, low and outside. Jill saw Dennis check his swing. Those were exactly the kind he liked to go after, she knew—those low balls that he could get his bat under and get out of the park. Now if the pitcher would only offer him something like that in the strike zone, she thought, they'd be in business. The next pitch was another ball and the one after that was a strike. The fourth pitch was the one Dennis had been looking for. Jill knew by the sound it made that the best part of the ball had made contact with the best part of the bat. The ball soared out over the field and even the center fielder's magnificent leap couldn't keep it from hurtling over the fence. The crowd was on their feet and cheering as the three runs came in to score. Jill screamed so hard that her throat hurt for hours.

Greenwood scored twice in the sixth inning and left the bases loaded in the seventh. Alta Vista picked up one more run in the bottom of the eighth to make the score four to two. In the top of the ninth the Alta Vista pitcher tired and walked a man who advanced to second on a stolen base. He gave up another walk and struck one out. A new pitcher came in, retired the first batter he faced, and deliberately walked Steve Reinhart, Greenwood's best hitter.

Jill clenched her fists so hard, she felt her nails digging into her curled palms. Bases loaded, two outs, and a score of four to two. Another walk would bring in a run and still give Greenwood an out to work with. A long single or a clean double would score two runs. A triple would clean the bases and give Greenwood a one-run lead. A home run would sink Alta Vista's spirits and force them to score two runs in the ninth just to tie the game.

Jill wished she knew more about Gary Wells, the Greenwood player who was coming to bat. She glanced across at Mr. Rhodes, who had kept a box score of the entire game. "What'd this guy do so far?" she asked.

Mr. Rhodes looked at her. "Struck out, grounded out to first, and a double."

Jill listened to the progression. She didn't like it—Wells's batting pattern was improving over the course of the game. Having doubled his last time at bat, he'd arrive at the plate full of confidence.

The first two pitches were strikes. Then, having worked ahead of the batter, the pitcher surrendered three balls. With a full count the batter had a definite advantage over the pitcher. He could foul balls back out of play all day, while the pitcher's arm just got more and more tired. Jill closed her eyes for a split second. Then she heard the sickening sound of the bat on the ball. It was the same rich, echoing thump she'd heard when Dennis hit his home run. She looked out toward the field, trying to spot the ball. It was a low line drive, and it would clear the fence by only a few feet. Dennis was back-pedaling

toward it, his glove arm extended. He timed his
jump at just the right moment, leaped up, got the
ball, and slammed into the fence. He bounced forward in a rough somersault.

Where's the ball? Jill thought, jumping up. Did he
hang onto it? Dennis got to his feet, his glove up to
signal that he still had the ball.

That was it—the third out. Alta Vista had won the
game. *Dennis* had won the game! Jill scrambled
down the bleachers and out onto the field. She had
to fight through the crowd to get to Dennis. When
she did, she threw both arms around him.

"I'm all dirty," he said, "and sweaty. You'll get
messed up."

"I don't care," she said. She didn't. She was so
happy, she would have rolled in the soft dirt around
the pitcher's mound.

All around them, people were shaking up cans of
soda and opening them, pouring the foaming liquid
over the heads of the victorious players. "I guess
they don't use champagne until you get to the major
leagues," Dennis said, and laughed.

A reporter from the local paper came up. He
wanted to interview Dennis about the game. Jill
stepped back and waited until they were finished.
Then Dennis came over to where she was standing
with his parents. "The coach says we look like pigs—
wants us to go home and shower before the party."
He grinned at Jill. "You look like you could use a
little soap and water yourself."

Jill looked down at her clothes. Her blouse was
soaked with soda and her bare legs, where she'd
brushed against Dennis's uniform, were gray with
dust. "I guess I got a little carried away," she said.

At the Rhodeses, Dennis and Jill took showers. Jill brushed the dust off her khaki shorts but her blouse was sticky with soda. Dennis lent her a clean shirt of his own to wear. It was too big for her, of course—she had to roll the sleeves up to keep the cuffs from sliding down over her hands. Still, she liked wearing the shirt. It was a little bit like having Dennis's arm around her.

She called her parents to tell them that Alta Vista had won and to tell them the party would probably last until eleven or so. She didn't want them to worry about her, and promised to be home before midnight.

The party got going around dusk, and was held in a park on the outskirts of Alta Vista. There was a big bonfire, plenty of food, and all the ballplayers and their friends. There was even an impromptu band. Several couples found a flat, grassy space and began to dance.

Dennis and Jill were sitting on the ground, leaning against the trunk of a fallen tree. "Want to dance?" Dennis asked.

Jill shook her head but it was too dark for Dennis to see her. "No," she said. "I really don't want to dance."

Dennis put his arm around her. "Me either," he said. Light from the bonfire flickered on their drawn-up knees. "So you liked the game, huh?" Dennis asked.

"I loved it," she said.

"Good," he said, his voice light and teasing. "Then you'll want to see every game I play this summer."

"This *summer*?" Jill questioned. "You *are* kidding, aren't you?"

"Nope. Summer league ball. Two games a week, twelve weeks in the season, that's—"

"Twenty-four games," Jill said.

Dennis paused. "Well, are you going to be there for them?"

Jill's voice was as light as his, even though her words were serious. "I don't know," she said honestly. "I mean, I've got to find a job and start saving some money for college. And I want to make time to write too. I haven't forgotten about that."

"In other words," Dennis said, his voice sounding disappointed, "you'll be too busy."

"That's not what I said," Jill corrected. "I just said there are some things of my own I have to do. After that, you're my next top priority."

Dennis didn't say anything at first. Then he leaned over and brushed her cheek with his lips. "I guess I can live with that," he said.

"Good," Jill said. She moved closer to him and settled herself against his strong, warm body. She had never felt the dizzying, head-over-heels feelings about Dennis that she had once felt about Toby Martin. But sitting here now, curled against his body, she felt she was in exactly the right place. Love was a sneak, she thought, coming up on you when you least expected it and surprising you with happiness you'd never even dreamed of.

The End

Jill waited anxiously for the opening announcements to be read on Wednesday morning. Mr. Daily, the vice-principal, began with the most important news first. "I'm pleased to announce that next year's senior class has a new president this morning. First, though, I'd like to congratulate the three candidates who ran, and every member of the student body who voted. We had an unusually high turnout this time, and . . ." Jill's fingers tightened around the Bic pen she was holding. The vice-principal went on about voter turn out and civic involvement in politics for what seemed to be hours before he came back to the important news. "In a very close election, Toby Martin has been elected president."

Jill let the news sink in. She had wondered how she would react if Toby won. But it was all right. She was glad for Toby, really *glad* for him. Jill was almost as happy to see that she was going to be okay as she was to hear that Toby had been elected. She spent the rest of her study-hall period making a congratulations card for him. She had only notebook paper with her, and her blue Bic, yellow Hi-Liter, and a red Flair pen. But she did the best she could, folding a piece of paper in half to make a card and writing CONGRATULATIONS in funny cloudlike letters that she filled in with stars, stripes, polka dots, and anything else she could think of. When it came time to write on the inside of the card, she wasn't so sure of herself. At last she decided on the simple truth and wrote: *If it couldn't be me, I'm glad it was you. Love*

Jill. She'd had to think a minute or two before writing *Love, Jill*, but it didn't seem right to put down anything else. She signed everything *Love, Jill*—even the letter she'd written to *Seventeen* magazine because they'd lost her subscription. She'd been thirteen then, of course, and had done it only because she couldn't spell *sincerely*.

Between classes Jill went to the third floor, where Toby's locker was. She wasn't sure exactly which locker was his, so she taped the card to the wall above the lockers, figuring that he'd find it. After all, how many people would be looking for congratulations cards that day?

The hardest part about the day was that people kept coming up to her and telling her they were sorry she hadn't won. They looked so sincere, Jill wished she could somehow explain to them that it didn't matter all that much. She was glad she'd run. She would have liked to have been elected, of course, but it certainly wasn't the end of the world. Before lunch she stopped in the office of the school paper to hand in an assignment. "I just wish I could print a huge ad saying, 'So I didn't win—so what?'" she complained to the editor, Lisa Valdez.

"Why?" Lisa asked. "Is everyone swamping you with sympathy?"

Jill nodded. "If everyone who's come up to me today had actually voted for me yesterday, I'd have won by a landslide. Everybody says they're *terribly* sorry I lost."

"You notice," Lisa said, "that I'm not saying that."

Jill looked at her. "Why not?"

"I've put a lot of work into the paper this year. I'd like to leave it in good hands."

Jill remembered what Lisa had hinted at weeks ago—that next fall Jill would be asked to be the paper's editor. She grabbed Lisa's hand. "Lisa, do you know something I don't know?"

But Lisa laughed and pulled away from her. "I know a *lot* of things you don't know," she said. "You forget, I'm a senior."

"I'm *almost* a senior," Jill answered.

"That's right," Lisa said. "Almost but not quite. Besides, you want to have a few surprises in store, don't you?"

Jill could tell by the firm set of Lisa's mouth that she wouldn't get any more information out of her. "Well," she said, resigned to the fact that she wasn't going to find out anything else, "it's food for thought, I guess."

Lisa glanced at the clock on the wall. "Speaking of food," she said, "isn't it time for you to go to lunch?"

Jill grinned. "Are you trying to get rid of me?"

"Yes," Lisa said, "before I tell you more than you should really know."

"I think you just did," Jill said, giggling. She stopped at the door and glanced back at Lisa. "Thanks," she said.

As she walked down the hall toward the cafeteria she thought about what it would be like to manage the school paper. Fun, she decided, and a lot of hard work too. Of course, she'd have to keep abreast of issues like student government. She'd have to know what the class president was up to. In fact, she decided, she'd probably have to cover the class president personally. *Very* personally. The thought made her smile.

Toby was waiting for her outside the cafeteria. "I got your card," he said, coming up to her. He was smiling, and his blue eyes were sparkling like twin lakes with sunlight pouring down on them.

"Did you like it?" Jill asked eagerly.

"I like *you*," Toby said, taking her elbow and steering her gently through the crowd. They dropped their books on a table to mark their space and got in line. Jill was quiet. Toby's words—*I like you*—kept playing over and over in her mind like a song. She was too busy listening to the song to talk. Finally Toby said, "I was watching you walk down the hallway. You had a big, beautiful smile on your face." He lowered his voice and leaned toward her, almost whispering in her ear. "I hoped you were thinking about me."

Jill looked at him. "Well, I was, in a way."

Toby grinned at her. "Am I going to hear the particulars?"

"No," Jill said. She didn't want to tell him that she was probably going to be the paper's editor next year. That was her secret—hers alone. She wanted to keep it that way.

But Toby looked dissatisfied. "Aw, gee," he said. "Just one little detail?"

"Why not let your imagination fill in the blanks?"

"That," Toby said, "could be dangerous."

"Uh-oh," Jill said, and laughed. "Then maybe we'd better talk about something more concrete."

They picked up silverware and napkins and paid for their lunches. After they sat down, Toby looked at her and said, "How about Friday night, then? We're still going out, aren't we?"

"You bet," Jill said. And because she was afraid she'd sounded a little too eager, she added, "I mean, if you still want to."

"Of *course,* I want to," Toby assured her. "And I want it to be special, a real celebration. How does this sound: I'll borrow my dad's car, and we'll drive over to Hermosa for dinner—they have a place where we can get lobster or shrimp or whatever you want—then we'll go dancing or something, okay? Mickey's Muggers are playing at the Bivouac. What do you say?"

"It sounds *delicious,*" Jill replied. "Which is more than I can say for this turkey and gravy. Ecch!"

"You're right," Toby agreed. "These potatoes are already starting to set. You know what? If they sold this stuff as Super Glue instead of food, they'd make *millions!*"

Jill spent the next two days looking forward to her date with Toby. It was good she had something to look forward to, because she didn't see much of Toby himself. He was busy getting things under way for next year—lining up people to work with him, talking to the kids who'd be involved in the student council. Jill admired his ambition. It wasn't Toby's fault, she reasoned, that he was so busy, she had to admire him from afar.

On Friday afternoon she was eating lunch with Pam when Nick asked if he could join them. He looked exhausted, and Jill asked if he'd just come from gym class.

"No," Nick said, "but I feel like it. I just had a meeting with our new class president—I feel like

I've been through the 'ground-in dirt' cycle of my mom's washing machine."

Pam laughed. "Oh, come on," she said. "It couldn't have been *that* bad."

Nick looked grim. "Want to bet?" he asked, taking a vicious bite of his food. "I just had to give him a rundown of everything—and I mean *everything*—the student council was going to tackle next year."

Jill found it impossible to keep her good feelings about Toby to herself. "Toby just wants to do a good job," she put in. "He's a very *organized* person."

Nick glanced at her. "Personally," he said, "I think you would have made a better president, Jill—you're human, you know how to have a good time, you know Rome wasn't built in a day. Toby's a pressure cooker. I mean, the guy's a *maniac* for getting things done. I think he could wear out a robot."

Jill didn't say anything. She realized that Nick didn't know how involved she was with Toby. That didn't surprise her—she and Toby hadn't even been out together yet. But that was about to change. Today was Friday, and tonight they'd have their first date. It was only a matter of time, Jill thought happily, until the whole school recognized them as a couple.

Toby was supposed to pick her up that night at seven o'clock. By six thirty Jill was dressed and ready. She had decided to wear her new pullover T-shirt dress. The dress was white, with big diagonal bands of red and black running across the front. She walked back and forth in the family room, looking anxiously out the window toward the road and listening to the sound of her new red sandals on the bare oak floor.

At five minutes to seven the phone rang. It was Toby. "Jill? Uh, hi. Look, I'm really sorry, but I'm going to be a few minutes late. I got tied up with something at school and completely lost track of the time. I'm just about to jump in the shower. I should be at your place in about a half hour, okay?"

"No problem," Jill told him. "I'll be here." She tried to sound casual about the whole thing, but she was disappointed. She hated waiting, hated walking back and forth in the family room when—if things had gone according to schedule—she should already be with Toby.

It was almost eight o'clock by the time he finally arrived. Jill had chewed her way through three applications of lipstick. "It's about time," she said. "I was beginning to think you'd changed your mind about me."

Toby shot her a dazzling smile. "Never," he said. "Not in a million years." He didn't mention his lateness until they were out on the highway, driving through the purple twilight toward Hermosa. Without taking his eyes from the road, Toby reached over and took her hand. "I hope you're not too mad at me to have a good time," he said, and gave her hand a little squeeze. "I mean, I'm really sorry about being so late. I just hope you'll give me a chance to make up for it."

"We'll see," Jill said, but her voice was light and teasing, and she slid closer to Toby in the car.

Toby glanced at her. His blue eyes were luminous in the dusk. "You mean," he said, "that things'll be okay so long as I'm on my best behavior?"

Jill laughed. He made her feel special. "Something like that," she answered, sliding even closer to him.

Riding with Toby along the smooth, flat gray ribbon of highway was so wonderful that Jill was almost sorry when they reached Hermosa. They drove through the town to its western edge.

"This is a great restaurant," Toby said as he parked the car. "Have you eaten here before?"

Jill shook her head. Not only had she never eaten in this particular restaurant, she'd never eaten in one even vaguely like it. The Golden Cactus was beautiful. There were filmy curtains of antique lace at the windows, candles in burnished brass holders, and fresh flowers on every table. The menus were bound in leather, with gold cacti embossed on the front. *Thank goodness I wore my new dress,* Jill thought, remembering that she'd almost decided on her beige jump suit and red scarf.

"What a great place," she said, smiling at Toby.

He smiled back, the candlelight making little sparks of gold in his eyes. "Glad you like it," he said.

Jill looked around. "It's so . . . so special," she said.

"So are you," Toby replied.

They ate spinach salads, broiled scallops, and potato skins stuffed with cheese. For dessert they ordered chocolate mousse. "That was *wonderful*," Jill said, licking the last bit of mousse from her spoon.

Toby chuckled. "Would you like another one? I'm sure there's more in the kitchen."

Jill shook her head. "No way. I'm absolutely stuffed."

"Let's just sit here a while, then," Toby suggested. He signaled to the waitress and ordered two cups of coffee. Jill hated coffee, but she admired Toby's sophistication in ordering it and drank it anyway. By the time they left Hermosa, it was going on eleven o'clock. Toby yawned as they climbed into his father's car. "Gosh," he said, "I didn't realize how tired I was."

Jill looked at him in surprise. "Too tired to go dancing?" she asked, remembering that they'd planned to go from dinner to the Bivouac, where Mickey's Muggers were playing.

Toby looked across at her. "Do you really want to?" he asked. "I mean, it'll be so late by the time we get back to Westmore, and I've got to get up early tomorrow and finish my term paper for world history."

"We don't have to," Jill said.

Toby reached over and touched her arm. "I'm letting you down again, aren't I?" he asked with an endearing smile.

"It's all right really," Jill insisted. Something was missing. Eating with Toby at the Golden Cactus had been fun—wonderful, in fact—but now the evening was going flat. It wasn't that she wanted to go dancing all that much exactly. Mostly it was just the way Toby was handling things. On the one hand he seemed to leave it up to her, whether they would go or not. On the other hand Jill felt the choice had already been made and it was her job to convince Toby that she didn't really want to go to the Bivouac, even though she did.

At the door of Jill's house Toby kissed her good night. "We'll go dancing *next* week," he said. "I promise." He kissed her again, pulling her close to him and holding her for a long moment before he let go.

What am I complaining about? Jill wondered as she let herself into the house. *I've just had a date with the most exciting boy in Texas, and he's asked me out again for next week. I should be as happy as a clam.*

Later that night, just as she was falling asleep, she wondered whether clams were happy at all. And if they were, how could anyone tell?

She managed to see Toby exactly twice during the next week at school—once for lunch and another time in the library. Now that he'd been elected president, he was throwing himself into the role—making notes on future projects, talking to his constituents to find out what was on their minds.

"I don't think the president of the whole United States is busier," Jill complained to Pam. "I wonder why there aren't lots of divorces in the White House."

Pam laughed. "I don't think it's the presidency that's at fault," she said.

"What do you mean?" Jill asked.

Pam shrugged. "I think that's just the kind of person Toby is. Whatever's around for him to get involved in, he will. He'll *always* be throwing himself into something."

Jill looked dismayed. All week long she'd been telling herself that things were only *temporarily* hectic. Eventually they'd settle down and she and Toby would have a nice, normal relationship. "I don't know, Pam. I mean, I hope it isn't true. If it is..." she stopped and frowned.

Pam finished the thought for her. "If it is, where do *you* fit in?"

"Something like that."

"Good question."

"Got any answers?" Jill asked hopefully.

"Nope," Pam said. "I guess time will tell though, won't it?"

But time *didn't* tell—at least, not quickly enough for Jill. Two weeks later she was as confused about Toby as ever. Whenever they did manage to spend time together, it was great. He was charming and wonderful and so much fun that he made Westmore, Texas, seem like the most exciting place on earth. The problem was, there was very little time to spend together. Toby was always busy—first with his presidency, then with his campaign to find the perfect summer job. "If you want to wait until school lets out," he told Jill, "all the good ones are taken." She admired his ambition and his philosophy—who wouldn't?—but that didn't make things any easier. On the rare occasions when they did manage to get together, it was because Jill managed to fit her schedule to his. She would rearrange her study times, put off doing something with Pam, or miss dinner with her family just to be with him.

"It's driving me nuts," Jill said. "I can't do *all* the compromising, can I?" She was sitting on Pam's bed paging through the May issue of *Mademoiselle*.

"Have you told Toby that?" Pam asked.

"I've hinted," Jill said.

Pam snorted. "You have to do more than hint," she said. "Believe me, I've had years of practice at this. Boys are a little thick sometimes. And they *definitely* hear only what they want to hear. Besides, why should Toby change the way he's acting?"

"To make me happy," Jill said innocently.

Pam looked at her pityingly. "You *are* a babe in the woods, aren't you? Look how happy you're making him—he's got exactly what he wants. Why should he change? I mean, look—you're practically falling over yourself making everything convenient for him. No, if you want him to change, you're going to have to do something radical. Something that'll really shake him up and make him think twice."

"Like what?" Jill asked. "I can't very well bomb his house, can I?"

Pam thought a moment. "No," she decided at last. "They'd probably arrest you for that."

"*Probably* arrest me?" Jill gasped. "Look, Pam, I don't know what you've got in mind, but—"

Pam grinned at her. "Just kidding," she said. "Wait. Hold it. I've got an idea." She tipped her head sideways to look at the open pages of the magazine. "What's that headline say?" she asked.

Jill read the headline, printed in pink ribbon above four girls in cascading pastel dresses. "It says, 'Dazzle Him at Prom Time.'"

"Exactly," Pam said.

Jill looked at her. "'Exactly' what? I don't get it."

"Prom time," Pam said. "It's less than three weeks away. Has Toby asked you yet?"

"No," Jill admitted, then added, "but I'm sure he will."

"Perfect. You see, that's just what I mean—you're letting him take you too much for granted. Good old Jill—you'll always be there when he wants you. *Don't be there*," she said. "That'll make him think twice."

"Yeah," Jill said. "It'll make him think twice about ever seeing me again."

Pam waved aside her objections. "So what?" she asked. "I mean, this way you aren't quite having a relationship, but you're not quite *not* having one either. Wouldn't you like something a little more definite?"

"Like spinsterhood?" Jill asked. "Suppose—just suppose—that I agreed with you, about not being so available. What should I do?"

"Go to the prom with someone else."

"I couldn't," Jill said, appalled.

"Of course, you could."

"But that's so—so *drastic*."

"You said yourself that you've already tried the gentle approach," Pam reminded her.

"Maybe I should try to talk to Toby again," Jill said.

"When it comes to boys," Pam said with authority, "talk is nothing. They only respond to action."

Jill thought about it. Pam *did* have a lot more experience handling boys than she did. And she was right about one thing—talking to Toby hadn't done any good at all. He'd gone right on expecting her to conform to his hectic schedule. Still, going to the prom with someone else seemed almost like an act of war.

"What do you say?" Pam asked eagerly. "Ready to try a new approach?"

"I'm ready to *think* about it," Jill answered. "I'll let you know what I decide."

If only Toby would call me tonight, Jill thought, *and ask me to the prom, that would take care of everything.* But Toby didn't. The next time she saw him, he was flying from school to a job interview. "See you tomorrow," he said cheerfully, stopping long enough to kiss her cheek. "Why don't you come over to my house about eight? I should be done with my homework by then."

"Sure," Jill said. "I may be a little late though. I've got some things to do first."

"Oh?" Toby asked, looking a little surprised. "What?"

"Just things," Jill said. *Things like deciding what I'm going to do about you, for one,* she thought.

♡

If you think Jill decides to look for another date to the prom, go to page 158.

If you think Jill decides to talk to Toby again, go to page 169.

*E*ven Pam couldn't figure out who the voters were leaning toward during the final days of the campaign. "Kathy's going to pull a certain small percentage of the vote," she said, "but not enough to have a real impact on anything. As far as I can figure out, you and Toby are neck and neck. It's going to be close."

"You're a lot of help," Jill said. The suspense was killing her. She almost wished Pam had predicted a sure defeat. That way, at least she'd *know* how things were going to turn out. But Pam remained uncertain right up until Tuesday, the day of the election.

"I guess we'll just have to wait and see," she said philosophically.

The ballot boxes were sealed at three thirty, and the votes were taken to the library. Tom Griswald, the current senior class president, was in charge of sorting out the ballots. The school's librarian, Mrs. Hargrave, kept a running tally of the results. The vice-principal and two teachers served as witnesses.

None of the candidates or their staff members were allowed into the library. They waited outside in two anxious little clusters, Toby's group on one side of the hall and Jill's group on the other. Kathy had made a brief appearance and gone home, wishing luck to whoever won the election. "I know it's going to be one of you two," she said. "And I know whichever one it is, is going to be a great class president." Jill had never cared much for Kathy because she had always seemed so stiff and intellectual. Now she didn't seem that way at all. She's just a little different, Jill thought. *If I win, I'm going to ask her to help me work on things.*

Jill sat beside Pam on the floor, backs against the glazed cement blocks of the wall, knees drawn up. She was wearing the same jeans she'd had on the night Toby came over, the jeans with the little hole in the knee. She pulled at the frayed threads, rolling them back and forth between her fingers.

"You ought to get those fixed," Pam said.

"Are you kidding?" Jill said. "These are my crisis jeans. Without that little hole, I'd have chewed my nails down to the second knuckle by now."

They'd been waiting for almost an hour when Nick showed up. He'd just come from a student council and wanted to know if there were any results yet.

"Not yet," Jill said, shaking her head.

Nick sat down beside her. "I guess I'll wait, then."

Jill glanced at him. "It may be quite a while," she said.

"I'm not going anywhere special," Nick said in his easy, relaxed way.

Jill felt the warmth of his shoulder next to her. It was like sitting next to a big shady oak tree. She looked at his profile, at his firm chin and slightly crooked nose, at his sandy hair and light eyes. "Thanks, Nick," she said.

"No problem," he said, turning toward her. His eyes were warm and sparkling. "We Irish have to stick together, you know."

Another fifteen minutes passed. Jill's bottom was falling asleep from sitting on the hard floor. She stood up and dusted off the seat of her jeans. "I'm going to get a drink of water," she said.

She walked slowly to the water fountain at the end

of the hallway. She wasn't really thirsty, but she thought the water might refresh her. Gathering her shoulder-length hair in one hand, she bent over the basin and sipped. She stood up, water dripping down her chin, and ran straight into Toby.

"Don't *drown* yourself," he said with a grin, and reached out to brush the water off her chin with his fingertips. "It can't be all that bad."

"I hate waiting," Jill said.

"Me too," he agreed. But he didn't look like he hated it at all. He looked as calm and happy and handsome as ever.

They walked back up the hallway without saying much. Before they separated and went back to their own sides of the hallway, Toby gave her hand a quick little squeeze. "Remember," he whispered, "win or lose, we've got a date Friday night."

"I remember," Jill said. She saw that Nick was looking at her. "Bye," she said.

They waited another half hour before the door to the library opened and Tom Griswald came out. Pam leaped to her feet. "Are all the votes counted?" she asked.

"Three times," Tom said, pretending to mop his brow. "Whew! It was a very close election."

"Well, who won?" Pam demanded. She was so impatient, she was practically hopping up and down.

Oddly enough Jill felt perfectly calm. It was all over—the voters had made their choice, and all the ballots had been counted. Win or lose, it was entirely out of her hands. And either way, she was happy— happy she'd had the experience of running.

But Pam was still bouncing up and down. So were several people on Toby's staff. They practically mobbed

Tom, demanding to know the results. He pretended to push them away from him. "Don't kill the messenger before he can deliver his message," he said with a tired little laugh. "I'm going to turn this whole thing over to the new leader of the senior class. Madam president?"

Madam president. The words took a long time to sink in. *Madam. Ms. Miss. Mademoiselle. Me!* A bomb went off in Jill's mind, sending thoughts whirling in all directions, like bright confetti. *I won,* she thought over and over again. *I won!* Then Nick was helping her to her feet, and Pam, who was *really* bouncing up and down by this time, was hugging her fiercely. Jill's cheeks felt wet, but she knew she wasn't crying. They were Pam's tears—Pam, who was so happy for her, she was crying. Jill couldn't think of a single thing to say. Everyone was looking at her. "Gosh," she said at last. "Thanks. I mean, I'm going to try to be the best president I can be."

That was when she looked over and saw Toby. His face was practically gray. He was smiling, but his mouth seemed to have been chiseled out of stone. It hit her then. *He didn't expect me to win,* she thought with a sense of shock. *Never in a million years. He was certain he could beat me.* It hurt her feelings that Toby had thought so little of her chances. Even so, she shook hands with him when he came over to congratulate her. "It could have gone either way," she reminded him. "Tom said it was awfully close."

"Yeah," Toby said tonelessly. "It could have been the other way around, I guess."

Jill leaned close to him. "And there's still Friday night," she whispered. "You owe me a date, remember?"

"I remember," Toby replied. "See you tomorrow, Jill." He looked at her before turning away, but there was no light in his eyes. Not even a flicker, she thought.

The next day, Toby was absent from school. "It's probably the strain of the campaign," Jill said, "catching up with him at last."

"Hmmph," Pam snorted. "Strain, my eye. He just can't handle losing the election. Toby's a great winner, but he's got to learn how to be a great loser too." Pam stopped, realizing that Jill was looking at her. "Sorry, Jill," she apologized. "I know how you feel about him, but well, I just call them as I see them."

Jill said nothing. In her heart she agreed with Pam. Fortunately, though, she didn't have much time to worry about Toby or his sudden and mysterious illness. The day was hectic from beginning to end. First she was plucked out of her first-period class and called to the vice-principal's office. He wanted to introduce her as the new senior class president at the end of the morning announcements. "Just say hello for now," he told her. "Maybe you'd like to come back at the end of the day, after you've had some time to collect your thoughts, and take a few minutes to talk about your objectives for next year."

"Thanks, Mr. Daily," Jill said. She knew she was going to like working with the vice-principal. "See you at—when?—around two twenty?"

"That'll be fine," Mr. Daily assured her.

"Oh," Jill said, "I almost forgot. Can I get a pass from you—to get out of last-period class?"

Mr. Daily laughed. "I almost forgot," he said. He pulled a blue card out of his desk drawer. Jill could see the words SENIOR CLASS PRESIDENT printed across the top and her name written into the blank space. "This is your *permanent* pass," Mr. Daily said, handing her the card. "Once everyone gets used to you being president, you probably won't be asked to show it much."

Jill looked at the pass. She'd never realized the class president had privileges like this. *Freedom!* she thought. No more dodging past hall monitors. "Thanks," she said.

Mr. Daily laughed. "Gives you a sense of power, doesn't it?" he asked.

"It sure does," she agreed. Then she remembered whom she was talking to. "Oh, don't worry, Mr. Daily—I'm not going to abuse it or anything."

"I'm sure you won't, Jill. I know you're going to make a fine senior president."

It took Jill most of the rest of the day to get used to the idea that she really had been elected president. She didn't quite believe it had all happened until she heard herself begin the afternoon announcements by saying, "Hello, this is Jill Farrell, your new senior class president." Then, for the first time, she felt like it was all true—she really was the class president.

When she got home that afternoon, there was a green vase on the dining-room table with six yellow roses in it. They were beautiful; so soft and bright, they seemed to be shedding light of their own. And best of all Jill knew right away that they were for her. There was a little white card beside them with her name written on it in green ink.

Toby! she thought, her heart beating fast. More than anything, she hoped Toby had sent the flowers.

That would make everything right again, she thought. That would make everything perfect. But somehow even before she picked up the card, she knew that the roses weren't from Toby.

And she was right. Inside the card there was a green shamrock with four leaves on it, drawn by hand and colored in with the green pen. *Luck to the Irish*, the message read. *Love, Nick D.*

She was holding the card when her mother came into the room. "I see you found your flowers," Mrs. Farrell said. "Beautiful, aren't they? I couldn't help reading the note. Who's Nick D.?"

"Someone nice," Jill said. Nick *was* nice, she thought. It wasn't his fault that he wasn't Toby.

"So where are we going to go?" Jill asked.

"Go?" Toby responded. "Go when?"

They were sitting together in the school cafeteria. Our first lunch together, Jill thought. Toby's mysterious illness had lasted two days. Today, Friday, was the first time she'd seen him since winning the election. She looked around the cafeteria, hoping everyone had seen her sit down with Toby. "On our date," she said, answering his question. "Tonight. You still want to go, don't you?"

"Uh—oh, yeah. Of course, I do," he told her.

Somehow Jill had expected a more enthusiastic response. She tried again. "Well, where are we going to go, then?"

"Anywhere you want," Toby said. "Tell you what. You're the president, you make the plans." He tried to grin as he said it, but his grin fell flat.

Jill didn't know what to say. It wasn't her fault she'd won, was it? She reached across the table and touched his arm. "I don't want to be the president when I'm with you, Toby," she said. "I just want us to have a good time together."

Toby didn't move his arm away from her touch, but he didn't reciprocate either. Jill tried to understand his problem. He was still disappointed over losing the election, she told herself. In time he'd get over it.

They decided to go to a movie, then out for something to eat. "I'll pick you up around seven," Toby said.

Jill made a quick mental calculation. Seven o'clock. Almost seven hours until her date with Toby. That would give her enough time to get ready, she figured. She hoped it would give Toby enough time to get over losing the election as well.

To Jill's relief Toby was in a better mood when he appeared at her door that night. "Guess what?" he asked as he guided her down the driveway toward his car. "I found out that one of my favorite movies is playing in town. *Harold and Maude*. Did you ever see it?"

"Uh-uh," Jill said, shaking her head.

Toby grinned. His grin flashed at her like a star falling through the twilight. "It's a great movie," he said confidently. "You're going to love it."

Jill did love the movie. It was funny, but it had meaning too—what her English teacher would call "content." After the movie was over, Toby suggested that they go to Galahad's. There wasn't much of a choice really—Westmore was so small that there were only four places kids could go to hang out. You went to McDonald's after school and when you were broke; you went to Christine's Steak Palace after the prom; you went to the truck stop outside of town when you were starving and wanted to pig out. Every other time, you went to Galahad's, which had nice deep booths and was poorly lit enough to be considered romantic.

Jill looked at the menu. "What are you going to have?" she asked Toby. "Any recommendations?"

Toby's face lit up. He loved being in charge—loved feeling that he was the one controlling the situation, Jill noticed. "Stay away from the fried clams," he warned. "They'll kill you. The spinach lasagna's pretty good though."

Jill folded her menu. "I'll have whatever you have," she said.

Toby beamed at her. A few minutes later, when the waitress came to take their orders, he said, "Two fried chicken dinners, please. French fries, creamy garlic dressing on the salads. Oh—and two Cokes. Large."

Fried chicken! Jill hated eating fried chicken in public because it was so messy. And fattening French fries and a nondiet cola—she'd gain a hundred pounds! Oh, well, she thought, it was her own fault for telling Toby she'd have whatever he was having. There was nothing to do about it now.

Throughout the dinner Toby kept entertaining her by doing imitations of Harold from *Harold and Maude*. When he pretended to choke on his food, he was so convincing that people at the next two tables looked at them with worried glances. Jill laughed, but she wished that she could tell Toby that he didn't need to keep performing for her. She would have been happy if he'd just been himself, the kind of quiet and gentle person she kept imagining he was.

She was carefully wiping the last of the fried chicken grease from her fingers when she heard someone calling her name. She looked across the room and saw Nick Donnelly. He was with two friends—Bill Torres and Marcus Webber—but he detached himself from them and came over to where she and Toby were sitting. Smiling, Nick made a low bow, pretending to doff an imaginary cap. "Good evening, madam president," he said. "Hi, Toby."

"Hi, Nick," Jill said. Toby mumbled a hello and took a big sip of his Coke.

Bill and Marcus came up behind Nick. Marcus was carrying a paper bag of takeout food. "We just stopped by to pick up some chicken," Nick explained. He looked at the bones on their plates. "How is it tonight?"

"Delicious," Jill said, trying to catch Toby's eye to show him how much she'd enjoyed the meal. Toby, however, was looking off in a different direction.

Marcus transferred the bag of food to his left hand and offered his right hand to Jill. "I haven't had a chance to congratulate you yet," he said. "I know we're going to have a great time next year, with you as president."

"Yeah," Bill said, entering the conversation. "Now about the question of *unlimited* skip days for seniors—"

"Oh, no," Jill said, laughing. "No business, please. Not tonight. I'm here to have fun."

They talked a few minutes longer. Or rather Jill and Nick and Bill and Marcus talked. Toby didn't say a word. At last Nick said they'd better take off before the chicken got cold, and they said good-bye.

Toby was quiet for the rest of the evening. Seeing Nick and his friends had spoiled Toby's good mood. "Is something wrong?" Jill asked as they drove home.

Toby shrugged his shoulders. "It's just seeing those guys, the way they came up to you. I mean, gosh, Jill, I know it isn't *your* fault. I like you and everything, but back there at Galahad's I felt like the royal emperor's concubine or something."

He'll get over it, Jill thought. We'll go out again next week, and it will be different.

But next week arrived, and Toby failed to ask her out. "I don't understand," Jill told Pam. "I mean, he says he likes me and everything. What's wrong?"

"He may like you, Jill," Pam said, "but he likes his own ego more. I hate to say I told you so, but—"

Jill looked up at her. "Go ahead," she said. "What did you tell me?"

"Toby doesn't know how to lose. He has to be the star every single time. No matter how much he likes you, he's never going to be comfortable going out with someone who's more important than he is."

"But that's ridiculous," Jill argued. "I'm *not* more important than he is."

"Toby doesn't see it that way," Pam said. "He goes around thinking that you're the winner and he's the loser."

Jill sighed. "Poor Toby," she said. And poor Jill. It all seemed so unfair. Especially to her. She hadn't done anything wrong, but she was being punished anyway. "Maybe he'll learn to see it differently," she said.

"Don't hold your breath," Pam cautioned. "Some people never learn things like that."

It was a good thing Jill didn't hold her breath, because Toby never called her again. For a few days they ate lunch together, but pretty soon even that stopped. Jill went back to eating with Pam, and Toby started eating with Kathy Sorensen, who had run against them in the election and lost. Jill could hardly believe it the first time she saw them together. "Will you look at that?" she asked Pam in disgust. "It makes me sick."

"Lovesick?" Pam inquired.

Jill shook her head violently. "No, just sick-sick." Suddenly a strange feeling came over her. She felt as if she were attached to a hot-air balloon that was rising steadily into the sky, carrying her along with it. It took her a whole minute to identify the feeling. Freedom—total, complete freedom. She looked at Pam. "You know what?" she asked. "I think I've finally gotten over my crush on Toby."

Pam grinned at her. "I knew you would," she said.

That night, while she was supposed to be writing her final paper of the year for English class, Jill thought about Toby. She had never had such strong feelings about anyone else before. It was funny, she thought. She had been so sure those feelings were real. All during the election she had been convinced that, beneath the surface of Toby's dazzling exterior, there was a quiet, gentle, and intelligent person just waiting to fall in love with her. She kept looking for that person, but she never found it.

It was difficult to admit that that person just didn't exist. Not in Toby anyway.

But that didn't mean that there wasn't a person like that, Jill thought. In fact, she suddenly realized exactly where she could find him.

She picked up the receiver of her white telephone, punched 411 for directory assistance, and wrote down the number she was given. She was only a little nervous, she told herself. Just enough to make it fun. Still, she hurried to punch the numbers before she lost her nerve. After two rings a masculine voice answered the phone.

"Could I speak to Nick, please?" Jill asked.

"Speaking."

"Hi, this is Jill Farrell. It—uh—it just occurred to me that I never thanked you properly for the roses. They were really beautiful, Nick."

"My pleasure," Nick said. His voice was warm and easy and sincere. Jill could picture his light green eyes and gentle smile.

"Well, I thought maybe I could buy you a Coke or something sometime. You know, to sort of say thank you. I mean, we could get together and talk and—"

Nick interrupted her. "Would this be for business reasons or personal ones?" he asked.

Jill hadn't expected anything so to-the-point. But there was no use backing off now. "Personal," she said, the word exploding into the phone in a breathless rush.

"In that case," Nick said, "I'll be right over."

"Really?" Jill asked. "Now? Tonight?"

"Why not?" Nick said. "Why should we waste a single minute?"

The skin on Jill's arms prickled with excitement. She didn't say anything until she heard Nick's voice in her ear again. "Okay?" he was asking.

"Okay," she said.

"See you in half an hour."

"Bye, Nick."

She hung up the phone and flopped on her back on the bed, staring up at the ceiling. Nick. Nick Donnelly. It wasn't a surprise that he had accepted her invitation—she had been fairly certain that he would. What *was* a surprise was the excitement crashing through her body. It was a wonderful, delicious feeling. And in just half an hour, when Nick came over, that feeling would get better and better. Half an hour—yikes! She had to get ready. And she had to find time, somehow, to call Pam and tell her the news. But, Jill remembered as she raced toward the bathroom, knowing Pam's sixth sense for things, she probably wouldn't be all that surprised. She'd probably insist that she'd known it was going to happen all along.

The End

Jill kept waiting for Toby to ask her to the prom. When another week went by, and he still hadn't said a word, she decided to follow Pam's advice.

"Just one problem," she told Pam. "What if nobody asks me?"

"Don't be ridiculous," Pam said. "You're popular—*some*body's bound to ask you. The important thing is, when Toby gets around to asking, tell him that you've already made plans."

"Even if I haven't?" Jill wasn't so sure she liked Pam's idea.

"Sure." Pam nodded. "The worst thing that could happen is that you'll have to accept a last-minute invitation."

"From who?" Jill asked.

"I can't know everything, can I?" Pam questioned. "Trust me. Even if it isn't with someone you particularly like, remember that you're doing this for your own good—*and* Toby's. This is going to show him that he can't keep taking you for granted. It's going to put your relationship on a whole new footing."

"Yeah," Jill said, "like over the edge of a cliff."

She wasn't one hundred percent sure Pam's idea was going to work. And she might not have had the nerve to go through with it if Toby had asked her to the prom in any normal way. But, being Toby, he didn't ask her in a normal way. Jill had expected him to finally realize that the prom was just two weekends away, apologize profusely for his oversight, and beg her to go with him. That wasn't the way it happened at all. They were sitting in the school cafeteria, and out of the clear blue sky, Toby said, "What color's your dress?"

Jill looked down at the navy-and-white striped miniskirt she was wearing. "Sort of an electric navy-blue and white. Why?"

Toby looked exasperated. "Not *that* dress," he said. "The dress you're wearing to the prom. I have to get my corsage order in."

Jill looked at him coolly. "Does that mean you're taking my dress to the prom?" she asked.

"No, silly, it means I'm taking you *in* your dress to the prom."

"I don't remember your asking me," Jill replied.

Toby looked puzzled. "I didn't? Gosh, I meant to—I made a note to do it, anyway."

How romantic, Jill thought. All of a sudden, she felt like one more assignment Toby had to get done on time. In the center of all the noise in the cafeteria Jill's voice was quiet and calm. "You know, Toby, sometimes I don't think you need a girlfriend at all—I think you need a personal secretary."

Toby pushed his tray away from him. "Now, what's that supposed to mean?" he asked. His eyes darkened to a hard steel blue. It took all of Jill's courage not to look away.

"It means," she said slowly, "that I can't go to the prom with you. I've made other plans."

"You *what*?" Toby asked. He was visibly shocked. "You've got to be kidding, Jill."

"I'm not kidding at all. How was I supposed to know you meant to ask me? So I—I went ahead and made plans of my own." She said it so convincingly that, for a minute, she almost believed it herself. It wasn't until much later that day that she realized the prom was only two weeks away and she had to find a date or miss out entirely.

Jill's search for a date had to be a clandestine one. She couldn't very well spread the word that she was looking, or Toby would know that she'd been bluffing when she said she'd already made plans. And that, Jill realized, would spoil everything. So she made quiet, discreet overtures to any boy she thought might not have a date yet. She even called up Nick Donnelly—on the pretext of getting math help—and asked him what his plans were. But Westmore was a small school. There were only so many available boys and so many available girls, and people got paired up quickly. Nick already had a date for the prom and so did every other boy in the class.

With her own hopes of attending the prom fading, Jill wasn't in the best of moods when Pam asked her if she wanted to go shopping for dresses. "What do I need a dress for?" Jill asked. "I'm probably not going anyway."

"Something'll turn up," Pam said cheerfully. "Or rather some*one*. Besides, you can at least come along and look, can't you?"

So Jill went. They began their search at the local J. C. Penney, went on to Sears, and ended up at Minty's, the only store in town that could really be called fashionable.

"Look at this," Pam said, holding up an apricot-colored dress with a sweetheart neckline and tiered skirt. Delicate ecru lace edged the neck, the sleeves, and each tier of the skirt.

"It's beautiful," Jill said. "Try it on."

Pam disappeared into the dressing room and reappeared a moment later wearing the dress. Beautiful as it was, it was all wrong for her. The apricot color made her skin look sallow rather than rosy. The full, ruffled tiers made her look even shorter than she was.

"What do you think?" she asked Jill.

"Well, uh—"

"My thoughts exactly," Pam said, grinning at her reflection in the triple mirror. "I look like a stuffed midget. This dress looks terrible on me." She paused on her way back into the dressing room and looked over her shoulder at Jill. "It'd look just right on you though. Why don't you try it on?"

"Well . . ." Jill looked at the dress enviously.

"Oh, come on," Pam urged. "You can always put it back on the rack."

"Okay," Jill agreed.

The dress fit her perfectly. And Jill knew, before she even saw her reflection in the mirror, that the color would be just right for her peach-tinted skin and cinnamon-brown hair.

"You see," Pam said when she saw Jill in the dress. "Was I right or was I right? The dress is you—it's perfect!"

A saleswoman came running up to them. "It certainly is," she said. "Will that be cash or charge?"

"I'm not sure I'm going to take it," Jill said.

Pam glanced at the saleswoman. *Let me handle this*, her look seemed to say. She drew Jill aside. "Look," she said, "I was saving this for a sort of last-resort move, but it looks like that's what it's going to come to."

"What are you talking about?" Jill asked.

"Well, I feel kind of responsible for the mess

you're in. I mean, I know I kind of talked you into turning down Toby's invitation. Not that I think it was a bad idea, you understand, but—well, I do feel bad about you not getting another date. So, well, I've sort of asked around and got this blind date lined up for you. If you want it, that is."

"Who is it?" Jill demanded. "I mean, it won't be much of a blind date. I know every boy within a ten-mile radius." Jill paused, a horrified look on her face. "It isn't Kent Cooper, is it? I mean, you wouldn't fix me up with him, would you?"

Pam shook her head. "I promise, it's no one ghastly."

"Well, who is it, then?" Jill persisted. "I *know* that all the decent boys are taken."

Pam looked away. "It's . . . it's a distant relative of Tim's."

"Oh, great," Jill muttered. "What's he look like?"

"He looks *fine*, I told you. Now, are you going to take him or leave him? I don't have to remind you that your choices are pretty limited."

Jill looked at herself in the mirror. The dress was beautiful, and she didn't want to miss her own junior prom. Still, the whole thing would be a lot more exciting if she were going with Toby.

The saleswoman came up to them again. "She'll take the dress," Pam informed the woman.

"Cash or charge?" the woman asked Jill.

"What?" Jill asked. "Oh—uh, cash." She turned back to Pam. "This guy better not be a jerk," she whispered threateningly.

Pam grinned at her. "Leave it to me," she said. "It'll work out."

Jill hoped Pam was right.

* * *

Jill looked at herself in the full-length mirror that hung in the front hallway of her parents' house. *No matter how things turn out tonight,* she thought, *at least I feel pretty. This dress is a dream.* Her sister, wearing jeans and cowboy boots and a Dallas Cowboys T-shirt ten sizes too big for her, watched Jill. "What time are they going to be here?" Penny asked.

"Eight o'clock," Jill answered patiently. It was at least the millionth time Penny had asked the same question.

"It's five after," Penny said. "Maybe they forgot you or something."

Before Jill could answer, she heard the reassuring sound of a car in the driveway. A few seconds later the doorbell rang. *Here goes,* Jill thought as she swung the door open. *Now I'll see what this blind date of mine really looks like.* But the only person she saw standing in the doorway was Pam. Jill tried to look past her, squinting to see out into the dark driveway. "Are the guys in the car?" she asked.

"Well, uh, no," Pam said.

Jill panicked. She clutched Pam's wrist. "Where are they?" she asked. "Are they still coming? Did he back out?"

"Calm down, will you?" Pam said, laughing and shaking off her hand. "They're going to meet us at the dance, that's all. That way, we'll have two cars at our disposal. I mean, in case we want to split up later or something."

Jill gave her an exasperated look as they climbed into the car. "I never thought I'd be getting picked up for my first prom by my best friend," she said. "Not that I don't like you, Pam—I just always pictured something a little more romantic."

"The evening isn't over yet," Pam reminded her. "Things could still turn out to be pretty interesting."

"With a distant cousin of Tim's?" Jill asked. "I'm not holding my breath."

The gym—which had been transformed into a fantasyland of blue and silver—was half full by the time the girls arrived. "I feel stupid walking in alone," Jill said. "Everyone else is in couples."

"We're a couple," Pam replied, her dark eyes gleaming. "May I offer you my arm?"

"Very funny," Jill said. She failed to see why Pam was in such a good mood, or what struck her as so funny.

Once they were inside the gym, Jill looked around for Tim and her date. Finally she spotted Tim. He was talking to Toby—*Toby*! Jill felt her knees turn to Jell-O. It had never occurred to her that Toby would ask someone else to the prom after she turned him down. But there he was, looking absolutely gorgeous in a dark navy tuxedo and sky-blue shirt.

"Come on," Pam was saying, pulling her by the arm. "I see Tim. Don't you want to meet your date? He must be around somewhere."

"I—I can't," Jill protested. "Not with Toby—"

But it was too late. Pam propelled Jill across the floor, practically into Toby's arms. "Jill," Pam said, "this is your date for the prom, Toby Martin."

Jill froze. Was this some kind of joke? she wondered. She looked at Pam and Toby and Tim. They were all smiling at her. "But—but you said you got me a date with some—with some distant relative of Tim's," she stammered.

"Toby *is* my relative," Tim said. "You have to go

through a lot of marriages and second cousinages and things like that, but somewhere along the line, we're related."

Toby stepped forward and took her by the arm. "I hope you're not *too* disappointed," he said, looking right into her eyes.

Jill saw the corners of his mouth turn up, the way they did when he was about to smile. She beat him to it and smiled first. "I'm not disappointed if you're not," she said.

Toby's blue eyes lit up. They seemed to give off a light all their own, Jill thought. "Disappointed?" he asked. "I *begged* for the job."

Jill glanced at Pam. "It's true," Pam said. "After you turned him down, he came to me and asked who you were going with. He had me cornered—I had to tell him the truth. Then he cooked up this scheme and swore me to secrecy."

"You mean you couldn't think up some convincing fib to tell him?" Jill asked. "You'd make a terrible politician, Pam."

Pam laughed and shrugged her shoulders. "Maybe," she said, grinning, "but even you have to admit that I'd make a pretty good matchmaker."

"Hmmm," Jill said. "I think I'll reserve judgment on that for a while. I haven't forgotten how this whole mess started, you know. I mean, I'm not going to name names, but I did get some pretty questionable advice."

Tim shifted his weight from one foot to another. "Are we going to stand here all night and talk?" he asked impatiently. "I thought we came here to dance."

Pam and Tim drifted off. Jill didn't see which

direction they went—she was too busy studying Toby's face. She'd almost forgotten what a nice smile he had, and how his eyes could change from the lightest blue to the blue-gray of a deep, mysterious lake. She stared at him for a long time, not even thinking about the fact that he was staring at her too. Neither of them said a word or made a signal. But, almost at the same time, they leaned toward each other. Toby put his arms around Jill and rubbed his cheek against her silky hair. She felt his lips brush the top of her head and heard him whisper, "Gosh, I'm so glad you're here, Jill. I mean, I got so upset when I thought you were going to be here with somebody else and—"

"It *was* a pretty dumb idea," Jill admitted. "Saying that I already had a date."

"No," Toby said, "it wasn't a dumb idea at all. When I talked to Pam, she told me how you'd been feeling about me—about my never having time for you or anything. I never meant it to be that way, Jill. Honest. I just get carried away sometimes. I know I try to do too many things, and sometimes the really important things get pushed out of the way."

Jill looked up at him. "Does that mean that I'm important to you, Toby?" she asked, never taking her deep blue eyes from his face. It took every ounce of courage she had to ask the question.

"*Very* important," Toby answered. "I didn't realize how important until you turned me down for the prom." He hugged her close again. "I don't want us to stop being together."

Jill snuggled against him. The ruffles on his tuxedo shirt felt stiff and scratchy against her cheek. "Me either," she said.

He lifted her chin up just enough to kiss her. Music was playing, and couples were crowding all around them, but neither of them noticed. They stood together for a long time without saying anything. Then at last Toby murmured, "So I guess this means we'll have to make some changes in our relationship, doesn't it?"

"I guess it does," Jill answered.

Toby looked down at her. "*Both* of us," he said. "I mean, I know I have to be more available, but you have to tell me when things bother you, okay?" He grinned at her, a sudden grin that was like the sun flashing from behind a cloud. "And if you tell me and I don't catch on the first time, smack me one, okay?"

Jill laughed. Toby slipped his arm around her waist. "Want to dance now?" he asked.

"Yes," Jill said, "but I want to say something else first. You're right. I *do* need you to be more available to me, Toby. But—but I want to tell you that I'm going to try to change a little too. I mean, I know how involved you get in a million other things besides me. That's one of the things I like best about you. So I'm going to try to be a little more understanding about that, okay?"

"Okay," he answered softly, squeezing her hand.

Pam and Tim, breathless from dancing, came up to them. "You two look like the cat that swallowed the canary," Pam said. "What have you been doing?"

Falling in love, Jill wanted to tell her—and would have, if they had been alone. But Toby answered first. "Compromising," he said, winking at Jill.

It was funny, Jill thought. Pam had asked them

what they'd been doing and she'd wanted to say *falling in love* when Toby said *compromising*. Or maybe it wasn't so funny. Maybe the two things were the same after all.

The End

Jill stood on the doorstep of the Martin house and rang the bell. Deep chimes—like the chimes on London's Big Ben, Jill thought—echoed through the beautiful two-story home. Each chime made her stomach flutter, and Jill fought the urge to abandon her plan completely. But no, she thought, she had made her mind up and she would go through with it: Tonight she would talk to Toby about their relationship.

"Hello, Jill," Mrs. Martin said, opening the door for her. "Toby's in the family room, I think."

Jill had been to the Martin house often enough to know her way around. Somehow, though, she never felt quite comfortable there. Her own house and the homes of most of her friends were attractive and comfortable. The Martin house, with its pale oyster-colored carpeting and expensive bric-a-brac, made her nervous. She was always afraid of spilling something or marring the perfection of her surroundings.

"Hi, Jill," Toby said, getting up to greet her. "Long time no see, huh? Gosh, things have been busy!" He took her hand and pulled her down beside him on the couch. He slipped his arm around her shoulders and started to kiss her. "Good to see you though. You kind of have a way of taking my mind off all those other things." Difficult as it was to resist him, Jill found herself pulling away. Toby looked startled. "Is something wrong?" he asked.

"*Wrong* is kind of a strong word to use," Jill said.

Toby looked at her. "I have the feeling *right* wouldn't be the correct choice either, would it?"

Jill nodded. Toby pulled his arm away from her. "What's the problem, then?" he asked. "Something at home?"

"No," Jill said, shaking her head.

"School?"

"Uh-uh."

Toby was growing impatient. "Why don't you tell me what it is, then?" he asked. "I mean, I don't exactly want to spend the whole evening playing Twenty Questions with you."

"I'm sorry, Toby," Jill said. "I don't want to make this difficult for you. It's just that—just that it's difficult for *me*."

"*What* is?" Toby asked.

"There's a lot of things that are bothering me. Things about us."

Toby folded his arms across his chest. "Things like what?" he asked. Jill saw that he was sincerely puzzled—and surprised. He really had no idea what was bothering her.

"Things like the fact that we hardly ever see each other," she said.

"I'm busy, Jill. You know that. There's next year to worry about, and lining up a good job for the summer. My dad thinks that I should start checking out colleges now instead of waiting until next year."

All the frustration Jill had felt over the past weeks came to the surface. "But we don't have any contact," she said. "You could at least call a little more often, couldn't you?"

"I'm not a phone person, Jill," Toby said. "I mean, you *know* that—I've told you a hundred times that I hate talking on the telephone. Besides"—he paused and smiled at her—"just because I don't get in touch with you doesn't mean I'm not thinking about you. I think about you a lot."

"How am I supposed to know that?" Jill asked.

Toby's smile was dazzling—so handsome, it made her want to cry. "Because I'm *telling* you so," he said with perfect confidence.

"I'm sorry, Toby," Jill said. "That isn't enough."

Toby looked astounded. "Oh, come on, Jill," he said. "You're not going to make such a big deal about a few phone calls, are you? I mean, if that's all it is—"

"That isn't all it is," Jill interrupted.

Toby leaned back against the couch. "What else?" he asked. "What else is bothering you?"

Jill looked at him. *Doesn't he really know?* she wondered. "What about the prom?" she asked.

"Oh," Toby said, "the prom. Yeah, I guess you would be wondering about that, wouldn't you? Look, Jill, I know I should have told you, but I'm not going to be in town that weekend. My dad lined up this job interview for me—there's a chance that I could be a summer intern at a Fort Worth brokerage house. I'm going to stay with my aunt in Dallas that weekend so I won't have to get up and drive to the interview."

"You're going to miss the prom?" Jill asked.

"I don't have any choice," Toby said. "Sure, the prom would be fun and everything, and I'd love to go with you—but this job opportunity is a once-in-a-lifetime thing."

Jill didn't say anything. She wasn't mad at Toby—how could she be? He was just doing what seemed right to him. But for the first time she realized what different people they were. "I wish you had told me," she said softly. "About the prom, I mean."

Toby looked apologetic. "I'm sorry, Jill. It's just that I'm not the kind of person who's used to including another person in his plans. I guess I never will be."

Jill tipped her head back, pretending to look at something on the ceiling. She was really trying to keep the tears from rolling down her cheeks. She took a deep breath, and in a minute the tears went away. "I guess that doesn't make our chances of staying together very good, does it?" she asked Toby.

He slid toward her and put his arm around her. Somehow it was different from all the other times he'd touched her. The magic electricity she'd always felt before wasn't there. Something had changed, Jill thought—in her or in him or, more likely, in both of them.

"I like you, Jill," Toby said. "I like you better than any girl I've ever known. And I'd like to go on seeing you. But I'm just not the kind of person who can become too involved with anyone else. Not right now anyway. I guess what I'm saying is, I like you too much to tell you that things will be different from now on, because they probably won't be."

She turned her face toward him. The look in his eyes was enough to break her heart. "I guess that's what I needed to know," she said.

Toby wasn't sure what she meant. "Shall I call you sometime, then?" he asked.

Jill shook her head. "Not for a while." She tried to smile, but had the feeling the smile was crooked and a little sad. "Not until I'm over you anyway."

Toby held her gently for a minute. Then he kissed the top of her head. "I'm sorry, Jill. You deserve someone who can give you a lot more than I can just now. When you find him, I promise not to be *too* jealous."

Toby walked her to her car. Jill was proud of herself—she'd managed to get through the whole evening without crying once. Not on the outside anyway. Inside, it was another story. She started the car, waved at Toby, and backed out of the driveway. She drove all the way to her house in perfect control. Then she parked the car in the garage, leaned her forehead against the steering wheel, and let out a choking sob. She cried for a good ten minutes before she went into the house.

At first it was difficult to see Toby at school. Every time Jill passed him in the hall or saw him hurrying toward a class, she felt her heart contract into a tight little ball. If only he had done something terrible, she thought, or had been mean enough for her to hate him. But he hadn't done any of that. He had only been Toby. It wasn't his fault that he wasn't quite right for her. Whenever she saw him, Jill would feel tears stinging her eyes, and she would start to remember the things about Toby that *were* right for her.

"I'm so *mis*erable," she told Pam one day at lunch. "I mean, I had no idea it would be this hard."

Pam looked at her sympathetically. "Poor kid. I keep forgetting this is your first really big-time love."

"If only I could have changed a few things about him—gotten him to want to see me more and spend more time with me." Jill sighed. "Then things would have been perfect."

"Boys aren't Tinkertoys sets, you know," Pam said.

"You don't pick the kit with the pieces you want and then put together your own model. They're human beings—package deals. Usually you have to take them or leave them because changing them—even a little bit—is like trying to melt a glacier with a book of matches."

"I guess so," Jill said, nodding glumly.

Pam glanced at her watch. "Look, I promised Tim I'd meet him in the library. You're going to be okay, aren't you? I mean, I know you're unhappy but you can be left alone, can't you?"

Jill laughed. "I'm not *that* bad off, Pam. I can certainly make it to my next class without having a breakdown."

Pam grinned. "Good. Then I guess you're not going to commit suicide while I'm gone."

"Only if I eat another mouthful of this chop-suey stuff," Jill said, stirring the coagulating sauce and rice with her fork. "It's absolutely *poisonous*." She looked at Pam, who was laughing. It was the first joke she'd made since she broke up with Toby, and it made her feel good. Maybe life would turn out all right after all, she thought.

But after Pam had gone, Jill realized she had nothing to do but think about Toby. No, she told herself, she couldn't keep thinking about him forever. She tried to remember what she'd thought about before she got to know him. Clothes. Makeup. Grades. Assignments. But school was almost over for the year, so there was no point thinking about that. And what good were clothes and makeup if you didn't have anyone special to look good for? Finally she decided to play a game she had played with herself as a child. She pretended that she was suddenly promoted to queen of the world and she could have anything she wanted. She had to change the rules a little bit though—she had to tell herself that "things she wanted" could in no way include boys, one boy named Toby in particular.

If I were queen of the world, Jill thought, *I certainly wouldn't be spending this summer in poky old Westmore, Texas*. Where would she go, then? She thought of all the places they'd studied in world history this year: Paris, Rome, Moscow, Tokyo—all the great, important cities of the world. Finally she decided she wouldn't go anywhere famous at all. She'd go to some little town in the Alps and live like Heidi, drinking goat's milk and eating melted cheese on bread. There certainly wouldn't be any boys *there* to break her heart, she thought. Jill smiled. She wondered if, once you had cared about a boy, you could go anywhere on earth and not think about him. Probably not. Boys, she thought, were a lot like olives. You always opened the jar meaning to have just one, but somehow it never worked out that way.

Suddenly she realized she was staring straight at someone she knew. And of course, it happened to be a boy. It was Nick Donnelly, in fact. He smiled at her, and in a few minutes he got up and came over and sat down beside her.

"You seem to be in a pretty good mood today," he said. "I was watching you and you were just staring off into space and smiling for the longest time. I wondered what you were thinking about."

"Olives," Jill said.

"What?" Nick asked, giving her a puzzled look.

"Never mind," Jill said with a smile.

"I haven't seen you much since the election," Nick said. "You seem to have been—uh—pretty busy."

Jill knew that he meant busy with Toby. "I *was* busy," she told him. "I haven't been lately though."

Nick's face lit up. "Really?" he asked. "Gosh, that's—I mean, maybe if you have some free time we can get together or something."

Jill looked at him and considered. Nick was nice, she thought. Really *nice*. She couldn't go on being Toby's widow forever, could she? If she did, it'd make for an awfully dull senior year. Besides, she realized, she was probably a born olive-lover. So she might as well take the cap back off the jar and see what was inside. "I'd like that, Nick," she said.

He smiled, but he looked away from her. She saw his fingers tap a secret, nervous rhythm on the knee of his blue jeans. After a minute he cleared his throat. "I—uh—I suppose you already have a date for the prom."

"No, I don't," Jill told him.

Nick looked at her. "Really?" he asked. "Me either."

But he was still shy, so Jill took the next step. She nudged him with her elbow. "I suppose we *could* go together," she ventured.

"That'd be great," Nick said. A special light came into his green eyes and he nudged her back. "After all, we Irish should stick together, shouldn't we?"

"Mmm-hmm," Jill said, nodding. "Just promise me one thing."

"What's that?"

"That you won't wear a green tuxedo with shamrocks all over it."

Nick pretended to look disappointed. "But I had

one all picked out," he protested. "Green socks, too!
I thought I'd look terrific in it. You wouldn't be able
to keep your hands off me." He winked at her.
"You're going to wear a green dress, aren't you?"

"Is there any other color?" Jill joked back. "I
might even dye my hair green, and wear green eye
shadow and green lip gloss."

"At least we'll get noticed," Nick said.

"Yeah," Jill agreed.

"That'd be fine with me," he said. "Getting noticed
with you, I mean."

Jill didn't know what to say, so she just smiled back
at him, which seemed fine with them both.

Jill didn't buy a green dress for the prom, of
course. Instead, she and Pam scoured Westmore
looking for the perfect dresses. When they couldn't
find anything they wanted, Jill borrowed her parents'
car and they drove to Fort Worth for a day of
shopping. *Finding* wasn't the problem there—it was
choosing. It seemed that there were enough beautiful dresses to outfit every junior and senior girl in the
whole country. Pam chose a turquoise dress trimmed
with pink. Jill's dress was white with delicate pink–
and–dark green flowers embroidered down the front.
The dress fit her like a glove, hugging her slim waist
and blossoming out into a full skirt. "Gosh," Jill said,
turning in front of the mirror and admiring the
rounded neckline of the dress, "this is terrific, isn't
it? It even makes me look like I have a bustline."

"You *do* have a bustline," Pam insisted.

"Well," Jill said, "I do, in a minimal sort of way."
She looked at her curving profile in the mirror again.
"Nothing like this though. What do you think?"

"I think Nick is absolutely going to flip," Pam assured her.

After they bought their dresses, they picked out shoes and earrings and makeup. Both of them had plenty of makeup at home, but somehow it seemed that only new makeup would do for the prom. By the time Jill put gas in the car for the drive back to Westmore, she was down to the last of her savings. "No doubt about it—I've *got* to get a job this summer."

"Me too," Pam said. "But let's not think about that now. Who knows? Maybe some high-fashion photographer will happen to be at the prom, see us in our dresses, and insist that we come to Dallas and begin earning a hundred dollars an hour modeling gorgeous clothes for him."

Jill laughed. "You know, Pam, sometimes you live in never-never land."

Pam sat straight up in the car. "It could happen. You never know."

It didn't happen, of course, but something just as wonderful did: Jill had such a good time with Nick that she didn't think about Toby once. He picked her up exactly on the stroke of eight, and her parents crowded into the hallway to take pictures of them.

"I feel like a movie star," Jill said when they finally got away.

Nick took her elbow and steered her down the sidewalk toward the driveway, where his car was parked. "You *look* like a movie star," he said.

"Thank you," she said, and smiled at him. "You look pretty good too—even though you didn't wear your green tux."

Nick looked wonderful, she thought. He wasn't dazzlingly handsome, but there was something nice and reassuring about him. He was tall and strong, and when she stood next to him, she felt very special.

The theme of the prom was "Through the Looking Glass," and the prom committee had worked hard to make the gym look like Alice's Wonderland. Cheshire cats grinned down at them. Mazes of green crepe-paper hedges hid an enormous papier-mâché sculpture of the Queen of Hearts. There was a large arching hoop covered with tinfoil that was meant to be the looking glass. Each couple stepped through it as they arrived, and the school photographer took their picture. "I bet my parents are going to want at least a dozen copies," Jill said.

"Mine too," Nick agreed.

"I wonder if Pam and Tim are here yet."

It took awhile for them to spot any of their friends. The gym was crowded, and everyone looked a little bit unfamiliar in formal dresses and tuxedos. Jill spotted Tim first, but it took her a minute to recognize him. Even though he'd been dating her best friend for a year, she'd never seen him in anything but T-shirts and his baseball uniform.

"You guys look pretty sophisticated," Jill said, walking up to them.

"Don't we though?" Pam said, laughing.

Tim ran his finger around the inside of his collar. "It's a good thing there's only one prom a year," he said. "This sophistication is killing me."

Pam glanced at Tim, then back at Jill. "That's my man," she said. "Mr. Jerseys-and-Cleats himself. To him *guillotine* and *tuxedo* mean about the same thing."

Tim pulled Pam toward the dance floor, leaving Nick and Jill alone. "Want to dance?" Nick asked, and Jill nodded. She hadn't expected Nick to be a good dancer, but he was. "It's my Irish blood," he said when she complimented him. "Isn't there a saying about Ireland being the land of poets and musicians, or something like that? I guess dancing calls for a little bit of both."

Later in the evening they drifted outside the gym, down a hallway, and out onto the lawn of the school. It was so dark, they could barely see anything. Now and then they heard rustling sounds as other couples passed them. "Watch your step," Nick said, putting his arm all the way around her. "The grass is kind of uneven."

Jill felt the heels of her shoes sink into the soft earth. "I'll be okay," she said, "as long as we walk slowly. I wonder who invented high heels anyway. Whoever it was, he was highly sadistic."

"Want to go back?" Nick asked.

"No," Jill said, putting her arm around his waist.

They walked halfway around the building to a place where it wasn't quite so dark. They were right next to the gym, and the light from the open fire exits filtered out across the lawn. There was just enough light for Jill to see Nick's face.

Without taking his arm from around her shoulders, Nick leaned up against the wall of the building. Jill leaned too, settling herself beside him. He tipped his head back and looked up at the sky. "Look at that," he said, pointing.

"What?" Jill asked, looking up. The sky looked like a vast piece of black velvet with loose diamonds scattered across it. It was impossible for Jill to pick out just one of those diamonds as being brighter than all the rest.

"That star to the left. I think it's a planet. Venus, maybe." He leaned close enough to her for her to follow the direction of his pointing finger. "See?"

"Mmm-hmm," Jill said, even though she didn't. She was too content to get into the fine points of astronomy.

They stood looking up at the sky for a few minutes, leaning against the wall. Then Nick moved his arm a little, and Jill was facing him, looking up into his green eyes. He played with a strand of hair that had fallen from the pile of smooth curls on top of her head. Jill felt shivers of excitement race up and down her neck.

"That feels nice," she said.

He touched her cheek with his fingertips, going over each angle of her face as if he were trying to memorize it. "*You* feel nice," he said. He stopped when his fingertips reached her lips. Then he bent his head down and kissed her. She kissed him back, putting her arms around his neck. When they stopped kissing, Nick was smiling at her.

"This is a terrific way to end the school year, Jill," he told her.

She smiled up at him. "End?" she asked. "I was hoping it was more of a beginning." And she knew from the way he kissed her again that it was.

The End